About the

The author has lived in England, France and he currently resides in America, so he is not actually sure where he is from or where he is going. All of his life he has been a geeky scientist and is proud of this fact.

THE MEANING OF IT

BLACK, MD

THE MEANING OF IT

Vanguard Press

VANGUARD PAPERBACK

A CIP catalogue record for this title is
available from the British Library.

ISBN 978 1 80016 374 4

*Vanguard Press is an imprint of
Pegasus Elliot MacKenzie Publishers Ltd.*
www.pegasuspublishers.com

First Published in 2022

**Vanguard Press
Sheraton House Castle Park
Cambridge England**

Printed & Bound in Great Britain

Dedication

I dedicate this book to the people I love, Cassia, Jake, and Graham.

Acknowledgements

I acknowledge the artistic skill of Ricardo Ferrari for the author's photo and cover page.

Introduction

Ian was not sure what "it" was: Jane was "it" but didn't want to be, Brian thought he was "it", Jose was always watching and waiting for "it," and Roy was simply an obnoxious asshole. Did they find "it?" Or does it really matter? Read on and find out.

Bland

Ian didn't care about it and wasn't sure what it was, but felt he was destined for something. Upon meeting Ian, the most noticeable thing about him was, well, nothing really. He was rather bland. No other word for it — he was quite simply mediocre in a rather unnoticeable way. Some people came into a room and one could feel their very presence. Ian came and went without disturbing anyone. He lived at home with average parents and average dogs. They all lived in a boring house in a boring suburb of New Jersey, called Bridgetown. Ian was in his parent's basement playing *Firelord*, one of his few respites from being bored. Indeed, Ian dreamed of becoming the Firelord. *Firelord* was his favorite game; with a flick of the controller, Ian could scorch his enemies to an agonizing death. Once they were reincarnated, they would (of course) become his supplicants and follow him into battle and do his bidding. If only life were as much fun. Ian lived at home because of debt. At Bridgetown High, Ian had excelled at science, so had dutifully earned an undergraduate degree and Ph.D. in neighboring states. During this time, he had consumed too much alcohol, smoked a little weed and occasionally got laid (but, not as much as he would have liked). Ian then got a job with a local biotech company, using his Ph.D, in molecular biology as credentials, and when not working, spent his time between boredom and *Firelord*.

Ian, to all intents and purposes was average — average height, build, and looks. However, more than averagely bored. He had always had a low boredom threshold and knew there must be something out there but was never quite sure where to look. Subsequently, with little direction of his own, he meandered through life just waiting for "it" to happen. The big problem was — what was it?

The "It" Girl

Jane Porrima was it, definitely it…

Definitely amazing, definitely beautiful, definitely smart, definitely successful, definitely outgoing, definitely charismatic, and definitely out of Ian's league. Jane was born with a gold (not silver) spoon in her mouth, glided through life effortlessly, and had casually picked up an undergraduate degree and Ph.D. from Harvard. As though this was not enough, her long blonde locks cascaded over her beautiful athletic shoulders only to be outdone by breasts that conjured up images of two ferrets fighting in a sack (think about this for a while) and a bottom that drew eyes like magnets draw iron fillings. Jane was… well… she was pissed off! Pissed off with life, pissed off with society, pissed off with being judged and quite lonely deep down if one cared to ask. Though of course Jane had a black belt in numerous martial art disciplines and would knock your teeth out before a person got anywhere close to asking.

Being perfect is not easy. All her life she had wanted to be accepted and loved for her faults, not admired and desired as an object. Things had gone bad early for Jane. Daddy was a successful hard-working businessman and Mom was an attaché (not a case, she worked for the Foreign Office), meaning she had been brought up by a succession of nannies and carted around the best schools in New York. She had everything, everything that is, except, warm memories of cuddles and just hanging out with Mom and Dad. Of course, they loved her, just in a distant "love you darling, will call/ text when I get there" kind of way. What she wanted was parent time; what she got was anything she wanted with a big bow. Initially she had tried the socialite scene, but quickly got bored of it and the groping. When bored, Jane did something about it. One day while flipping through the channels on her incredibly large and "best there is" TV, she stopped on a science channel. Jane had excelled at science at high school, but then she excelled at everything. At Harvard she had majored in business studies, so that at least she could have some time chatting with Daddy. A bespectacled doddering old scientist was describing, what could only be described as love, for his theory. It wasn't so much the topic that had captured Jane's interest as it was the words he used.

"When one embarks on a scientific career, it levels us all to the same playing field. We do not know the answer, we do not know where we are going, even though we may think we do. We just know something is out there worth investigating. Everything in scientific research is a jump into the unknown. We predict, we make theoretical models, we hypothesize, but at the end of the day at some point we jump...

"At the point we jump, we all start from the same place. Man/woman, black/white, rich or poor, we all start with the same question — what if? Where you take that question and how you try and answer that question becomes a personal test of who you are. What others think of you and what others want of you becomes irrelevant. As a researcher, you make your own way on a quest to answer 'what if.' If you want to only compete against the unknown, this quest, and I mean quest, is for you."

Jane placed an elegantly manicured fingernail on the pause button. All her life she had endured privilege. Money and looks were in plentiful supply, she couldn't even play the dumb blonde card — too smart for that — and even when it came to competition she excelled naturally. She had represented Harvard at swimming and soccer ("Soccer! — Oh why, darling. it's so… close to other people and rough. Really?" her mother had proclaimed. "Oh, like you care," had been the reply before the phone went dead). So, competition came naturally. Even during black belt training, when lecherous Dan had "shown her a hold" only to take a quick grope of her breast, and she had extracted herself from him by lodging his left testicle somewhere around his kidney. Competing against others was boring. Why? Because she was always privileged by genes or circumstance. Being a woman had in theory thrown some obstacles in her way but most men simply melted under her charm so even this wasn't an impediment. Now, competing against herself — this was a challenge!

"Mmmhh, fuck it."

Jane changed her major to biology, and of course excelled.

Knox

Knox Pharma nestled itself between two major New Jersey highways, had easy access to major airports, and if the marketing were to be believed, it employed only the best scientific minds and had a future that could only be described as meteoric. The large glass façade and tasteful landscaping of Knox HQ only added to the aura of success. As one entered the reception, a smiling security guard, partly obscured by potted plants, enquired as to your business, made a call, looked earnestly at your ID, smiled again, and asked you to take a seat.

Jose cherished his job, and although it was a little monotonous at times, he was happy not to be cleaning cars or asking patrons, "Do you want fries with that?" Jose appeared to meld into the fabric of the company. He was thirty-ish, a little overweight, and very pleasant, always smiling, and had won a number of good employee awards. Beneath the surface, Jose had more than one might expect going on. He watched everything and knew everything. Jose, born Jorge in Colombia, had always suspected there was more in store for him than poverty. What little teaching had occurred during Jorge's life had shown a keen mind and logical brain.

As a young boy, Jose was quiet, sensitive, and somewhat of a bookworm. Quite naturally this led to him being bullied. Nobody likes to be bullied. Jose detested it. The kids in the village tormented Jose and he frequently came home bloody and beaten. What the kids didn't know was that when Jose did not like something, he did something about it — he read. Jose found books at the local library on self-defense and absorbed them. The kids in the village stopped bothering Jose. Indeed, a couple of kids disappeared, never to be seen again. No one ever suspected Jose and Jose never uttered a word, but sometimes he would catch his grandmother watching him out of the corner of her eye. No other trouble befell Jose and he continued to do well in school, even winning prizes for his achievements. Indeed, one of his most treasured possessions was a Parker pen given to him as a prize for his studies. School was not a priority in his village; farming was. The problem was farming was not, as far as Jorge was concerned, in his future. After his grandmother died, he kissed his mother and said he was going to make something of himself.

As a young man, he had made his way to the US border, paid smugglers to get him over the border and subsequently been stiffed on his life savings. The smugglers did not bank on Jorge's determination and although he did not give the impression, he was *not* a person to be crossed.

Armed with only a ballpoint pen, he had confronted the men behind a cantina in Santa Ana. Disarmed by the boyish profile and meek demeanor, the first smuggler had shown genuine surprise when the pen penetrated the eyeball with such force it came to rest in the region of the temporal cortex. Jorge, being right-handed and very attached to his beloved pen, twisted his body to the right in order to extract his prized possession. The brain of the first smuggler had reacted to the trauma by attempting to lay the body supine, thus collapsing the legs. This brought the weight of the body down onto Jorge's arm and pen. To counteract, Jorge dropped his hip and arm, twisting further to extract the pen, with quite a satisfying "slurp" sound. The coiled body posture required for pen extraction placed Jorge in a fortunate attack position.

The second smuggler had initially stood open-mouthed at the carnage taking place in front of him, but now moved to retrieve a switchblade from his pocket. As the "kid" had not looked anything like dangerous, he hadn't even bothered to check the blade — big mistake. The coiled tension in Jorge now released, swinging his body left and forward. His right arm shot forward and once again the pen pierced flesh, as the second smuggler was taller, this time in the throat, just in time to stifle a "what the f…" In a manner similar to a botched tracheotomy, the Parker pen pierced then traversed right through the trachea, coming to a hard stop on one of the cervical vertebrae. This time the pen was retrieved more easily and Jorge stood looking at the bloody scene in front of him. Both injured men were thrashing on the ground and Jorge became aware the noise might attract unwanted attention. A rusty spade laying against the wall of the cantina silenced the scene. Jorge cleaned his pen on the shirt of one of the smugglers and was pleased to see the damage was minimal. He took what money he could find on the smuggler, then looked into the distance.

Mmhh, north, he thought.

Jorge walked off North, washed in a nearby river and made his way to the land of plenty. His name had been used a couple of times at the cantina so along the way Jorge became Jose, the J a necessity of the "JP" engraving on the pen. Jose made his way in the world, always watching and waiting for something or "it" to happen.

"Thank you, sir, please take a seat," Jose indicated to the visitor and dutifully noted his name in the visitor list with his Parker pen.

The visitor was not kept waiting long. One does not keep one's benefactors waiting. Even for a rude bastard like Roy Knox. Roy had a flair. A flair to sell an idea, a flair to notice (and steal) other ideas, and a flair to make everyone around him want to vomit. Roy had scraped through a medicine degree at the University of Pennsylvania (U Penn as he liked to call it) and meandered into a research role more as a way of paying the bills rather than having a passion. Clinical medicine had not been Roy's forte. His bedside manner being so brisk and downright rude, he caused a wave of complaints and hypertension wherever he went. The molecular biology labs at U Penn had provided a less patient-intensive path for Roy, and all parties were happy with this. It was here that Roy found his niche in life. For limited periods of time, Roy could be charming and persuasive. He soon found out that this charm could unlock the thoughts of his fellow much smarter researchers. Having noted an as-yet-untested hypothesis of his colleagues, Roy, with a little nip and tuck of the idea, plus a leap of faith, proposed the idea, performed a quick confirmatory experiment and lapped up the praise of his faculty and peers. None of his colleagues were ever even so much as mentioned in his scientific breakthroughs, leading to resentment, anger and the occasional threat of violence. Roy, however, didn't care and moved up the chain of seniority quite quickly by making full professor by his early thirties. Any challenges by colleagues were quickly brushed under the carpet or simply ignored, his increasing seniority making it quite impossible to dispute him. Roy had a way of lying that made his words seem like the truth. No matter what trouble Roy got himself into he could talk his way out of it.

Having made it to the top of his ivory tower, the thrill of the climb and the beating of his colleagues became a distant, although rather enjoyable, memory. By his mid forties, the hair that was left on Roy's head was going grey, his off-the-rack chinos were too tight around the waist, and boredom started to creep in. Roy had never married, as loving someone else other than himself was a notion so foreign it never occurred to Roy. In his early years, Roy used his seniority, a little charm, and downright gall to fondle, caress and even have the occasional intercourse with several female students. These dalliances (as he liked to think of them) had usually been far from consensual and gave him somewhat of a reputation. This fact caused many female students and faculty to give him a wide berth. Indeed, the boredom, the lack of chances to molest female colleagues, and a rather unfortunate accusation of groping by the chancellor's wife had pushed Roy into thinking of exploring pastures new.

For all his faults, initiative and courage were not lacking in Roy Knox. Foresight and cunning with a healthy dose of entrepreneurial flair were also part of Roy's repertoire. The 1990s had been designated the decade of the brain by President George H.W. Bush and the biotech boom was about to take off when Roy hatched his plan.

Phosphatases are a group of enzymes that remove phosphate from proteins. Roy had pioneered (on the backs of others) work on a special set of these enzymes, often referred to as the "Knox phosphatases." This name was a great source of pleasure for Roy and rancor for his colleagues. Roy had convinced, rather too easily, a bunch of venture capitalists to back him in forming

Knox Pharmaceuticals. Together they were going to cure Alzheimer's disease, cancer, and well darn everything really, making them a thing of the past. So far, the company had about a hundred employees and a building with a nice glass façade that was surrounded by wonderful landscaping. All this was held together on the promise of success and scientific breakthroughs just around the corner. Hence the visit from the damn venture capitalists.

"Roger! How are you? Great to see you!" bellowed Roy as he strode confidently across the atrium, arm outstretched in anticipation of pumping his benefactor's hand (and of course pumping Roger's group for more money).

Roger Pimsbury, looked like his name, a stiff-arsed Brit, scared of his own shadow. As an accountant for a major law firm in "the city," he had made obscene amounts of money and figured he could be just as smart in another business. Having just started his own United Kingdom-based venture capital firm with some of his chums and rented a couple of offices in the town of Hedon, on the High Street just above Madge's Florist, Roger went looking for the next big thing. The fledgling Knox Pharma, nestled in the rolling hills of New Jersey, USA, had caught his eye with its outlandish statements on potential and he was bowled over by the brash confident yank at its helm. He really had no idea what Roy was talking about, but just knew it was "big", and he had to get in on the ground floor. Ever since, he had written Knox Pharma very large checks, but had yet to see a return on his investment. He was, however, starting to get a little worried. Five years ago, he couldn't open his checkbook quickly enough, but the "nearly there" statements and "just wait and see" were wearing a little thin. Roger was a realistic, but firm chap and he had bloody well had enough of being ignored and sidelined. Besides, the amount of money both he and his chums had dropped into this damn venture had given him frequent bouts of diarrhea. On one such occasion, he had not quite made the "lavvy" in time, forcing Roger to make an unscheduled visit to the Marks and Spencer's men's underwear section. This simply was not on, and quite frankly downright rude, he, Roger Pimsbury, was going to give this bloody Yank a good dressing down. The problem was his rehearsed speech had gone great on the plane and the hotel room; in person, however, he couldn't get a bloody word in edgeways.

"So you see, Roger, although we have had some minor hiccups, the rocket is just about to fire. Whoosh!" exclaimed Roy, thrusting his hands into the air.

Roy was in full charm mode as he leaned back in his very expensive, and monogrammed, leather chair. He had designed the office himself. The floor graded slightly upwards towards the impressive oak desk and all the guest chairs were lower than those of the boss. The view from the picture glass windows was lovely, starting with the research and manufacturing buildings (all mainly paid for by Roger and his chums), continuing over the ever-so-useful main artery highways to international airports and extending into the green lush NJ countryside that could be followed all the way to the Pocono Mountains. Roy loved being the boss, loved everything about being the boss at Knox and just needed this limey needle dick to keep writing the checks. Leaning towards Roger and breaking wind almost imperceptibly, he eyed his benefactor. "So, what do you think?"

Moving uncomfortably in his chair, Roger did not look as combative as when they had first met. There was also a bit of a smell in the air. "Could I just use your bathroom, old chap?" Roger scurried off in search of the bathroom.

As Roy ushered Roger out the door, grinning and back slapping all the way, he was not as confident as he appeared. He might have slithered away from Roger this time, but something about the limey's demeanor told his acutely tuned antenna that he was pushing his luck. *You better go rattle some cages,* he thought to himself. Roy spent most of his time in his new office or playing golf. Occasionally, however, he decided to "rough it" and visit "his people" in the labs. Indeed, that cute little blonde thing, Jane he thought her name was, had just started; visiting the labs would be a great chance just to see that cute little ass. Visiting the lab for Roy was like the king visiting his subjects and bestowing upon them his royal wisdom and judgment. Most people ran when they saw Roy coming. He was the boss, but he was also a pain in the ass. For some female technicians on occasion quite literally so. As they bent over their equipment, Roy always seemed to be reaching for something behind them. Of course, Roy had slithered away from any legal hassles and the three women who had lodged HR and legal complaints were left with no job and frequent nightmares about creepy old men.

The head of the lab was called Tang. Tang was well-educated, very smart, a wimp, and a complete supplicant to Roy. Just the sort of person that Roy had climbed on the back of all of his life. Indeed, many of Roy's scientific discoveries had started as Tang's brainchild. Tang was as meek and mild as Roy was brash and brazen. He had been with Roy for a long time; indeed, Roy had been Tang's Ph.D. supervisor. Roy had seen the potential in Tang. An extremely bright scientific mind who worked long hours without complaining, he was a brilliant conceptual scientist with no confidence of his own, the perfect running mate for Roy. Tang had never known anything else — he had always grown up and been taught to respect his elders and for him was just natural. Roy had been like a father and mentor to him, always there to suggest ideas and provide support. He had ignored the jibes from peers who had said Roy was using him. Tang had come from lowly roots and was now a prestigious scientist alongside the great Roy Knox. He owed him everything and would always be loyal. The only time his loyalty had wavered was when Roy had buggered him while drunk at a conference. The next morning Roy had apologized profusely, blamed it on drink and said he just wanted to "try it." Roy had firmly told Tang that it would not happen again, besides he didn't really like it. That was enough for Tang. Although, occasionally after straining in the bathroom after a large dump, Tang still bled from his anus.

"Professor Knox-san, what a pleasure it is for you to come visit us," said Tang mildly, accompanied with a slight differential bow.

Roy was never one to mince words. "We need to show some fucking progress, Tang. Those limey wankers are getting impatient."

"Professor Knox-san, we are making great progress. This is a good time for you to have come down. Come to my office and let me show you what we have recently discovered. It is quite exciting, sir."

As Tang scurried away, beckoning for his mentor to follow, Roy meandered after him. Roy never walked fast if he didn't have to. He had always found that watching, listening and being aware of his surroundings had provided useful fruit. Today was no different — it provided a peach.

"Well, hello, who are you?"

Jane was bent over a box of pipettes. Roy had a perfect view down her open lab coat and blouse an amazing cleavage, hemmed in by two lovely tight breasts. Roy's groin started to stir.

Standing up, Jane noticed Roy leering down her blouse but that was par for the course for Jane. The other lab colleagues had warned her about Roy. "My name is Dr Jane Porrima, and you are…?" Jane had had many powerful men look her over and make judgements and had received syrupy, lecherous advances all her post-pubertal life. She knew exactly who this old creep was. She knew exactly what he was thinking, and she was fucked if she was going to be subservient (and masturbation material) for yet another old guy who just assumed he "had the power." Even if he was the boss. She was good, she was smart, hardworking, and wanted to be accepted for her brain, not her tits and ass. This was a good opportunity for Jane to excel as a lead scientist at Knox, and prove her parents wrong about her career choice. However, if this creepy old fart so much as touched her inadvertently, she would knock his teeth out. Her martial arts training and surprising strength for someone so small and cute had sent more than one guy to the emergency room for reparative surgery. Jane shot out her hand.

Roy, quite bemused that someone did not know who he was, quite sheepishly took the outstretched hand and mumbled "Roy Knox. I…" He was even more shocked when this cute little thing pulled him down to herself with a surprisingly strong handshake and looked him in the eye.

"Ah, of course, the great Roy Knox, pleased to meet you," sneered Jane. "I have just joined from

Harvard and have some ideas I need to discuss with you."

"Yes… eer, of course… pleased to meet you, Dr Porrima, Jane, I…" mumbled Roy. He was quite taken aback by such forward behavior from a female, especially such a cute one, and for one of the first times in his life, he was speechless and not in control. He had also lost his impending erection.

"However, I see Dr Tang wants your attention." Jane cut off Roy's blithering. "So later then." Jane turned around, bent over to pick up the box of pipettes, paused just long enough for Roy (and the rest of the lab) to take in her perfectly proportioned buttocks under the lab coat and strode confidently off down the lab.

Liz Cammand, a technician who had worked at Knox right out of college and had been groped by Roy once or twice, had watched the whole thing in jaw-dropped awe. She had noticed Jane's looks — who didn't and made quite sure Jane knew what sort of person Roy was during their "let me show you around session." Liz didn't hate Jane for her looks as some women did. Liz didn't care. "You take me as you find me or fuck off" was an often-used phrase from Liz.

"Oh my god! Oh my god! Did you really just do that? I can't believe it." Liz followed Jane around the corner and they both hurried to the ladies' room, tittering all the way. "Oh my god, I have never seen anyone deal with Roy on that way. I fucking love you. Seriously, I fucking love you." Liz and Jane were holding on to each other in the bathroom lest the laughter brought them both down. "I am serious, I love you. If you want me, I will become a lesbian and fuck you right now, I will." Liz was gushing out the words, only stalled by bellows of laughter. "I would never have the guts to say something like that, you are my hero," shouted Liz.

"Ssh, someone will hear," said Jane, barely holding in the laughter. "No need, not into women, sorry, I prefer dick.

Yeah, me too," said Liz. "Shame that the dick is attached to the brain of a man. If we could just remove that."

"I hear you, take the brain, stupid mouth, and ego away and just leave the dick. Perfect."

"Was I really that good?"

"Oh Jane, you were magnificent, never have I seen that prick humiliated like that. Oh my god you were magnificent, you were ethereal, you were... I need to pee."

Both women relived the incident through the stalls while relieving themselves. A strong bond of friendship was forming as they left the bathroom.

"I fucking love you, Jane," whispered Liz as they walked back to the lab.

Both women were still giggling as they returned to the lab.

Roy had followed Tang, rather subdued and feeling that he had just missed something, but what? He sat in

Tang's office listening inattentively to his supplicant's exclamations.

"Now, talking about a big dick with a big ego, did you meet Brian yet?" Liz said to Jane on the corridor.

"No."

"Gorgeous, big muscles just the way I like them. Mmmhh tight butt cheeks, blue eyes… and a complete prick. A great candidate for brain removal. I think he comes back from vacation tomorrow." Jane was really getting to like Liz. She loved a woman who just spoke her mind.

Brian

Benjamin Wilkes ("Brian") didn't *think* he was "*it*" — he simply was "it." Born with a gene-set to die for, of course he was "it". Brian was tall, handsome blue-eyed, athletic and remarkably smart for a "jock type." He had coasted through life effortlessly, was adored wherever he went and thought everybody had it as easy as him. The only thing lacking about Brian was he had never really had to try hard at anything. Having an easy life had a downside. Never having to try meant Brian lacked drive. Sure, he always succeeded, but only just. However, that was enough for Brian. In Brian's mind, superficial was okay. His superficial looks served him well and his relationships with everyone apart from his mother (a mutual adoration and almost oedipal relationship) were also superficial.

Through high school and college, his charm and looks had supplied a steady stream of beautiful, talented young women on an as-needed basis. He was, according to himself, also amazing in the sack. However, a regular pattern had emerged. Once the novelty of the looks and charm had worn off, Brian found himself trying to answer unanswerable questions from these unfortunately very intelligent and "don't bullshit me" type of women like, "Why don't you connect with me?" and "I want our relationship to be on a deeper level, can you be there for me?"

Usually his bewildered answers like, "I am trying to connect. I can deep inside you right now if you want," were surprisingly not the correct answer. The occasional tear and slapped face marked the end of this chapter and Brian simply moved on. It was not that the ending of a relationship hurt him; it just left him confused. This confusion however was quite quickly forgotten when the next set of yoga pants came jogging into view.

Brian had had a wild time on vacation in Atlantic City. Most of his old college football team had turned up, and yes, quite boringly, Brian had been the team's quarterback. Much beer had been drunk, strippers had been purchased, fines paid by Mom ("sorry, Mom, it was the others, not me," "I know, Benjamin, you are a good boy") and really a rather good weekend ensued. Still suffering a little from a hangover and a day later than expected due to a night in jail (out thanks to Mom), Brian breezed into the lab. He stopped abruptly and thanks to his athletic prowess, darted behind a large freezer just in time before Roy and Tang could spot him coming in late. Brian did notice, however, that Roy was not strutting around like his usual peacock but with a shuffling demure amble. *He must not be feeling well*, thought Brian. Brian liked Roy. He was great fun. They often golfed together, and Roy always bought the drinks. Indeed, rather strangely, Roy had invited himself along on a few outings in the local college town. Although Roy looked a little out of place in a bar full of twenty-somethings, he was the life and soul. Frequently buying pitchers of beers, making jokes (surprisingly rude for an old man) and always offering to help drive people (young women) home. There was talk that some of these young women woke up passed out and naked and unable to remember a thing. Some had even made accusations against Roy, but Brian didn't believe any of that garbage. Roy was a good guy. Besides, those women had just been drunk.

"Hi Liz, did I miss anything, I... . oh hello, you must be new." Brian immediately fixated on Jane, forgetting Liz was present.

"You missed the best put-down of that prick Knox yet," Jane interjected, conscious of Brian's leering at Jane.

"Oh, Roy's okay. He is just a bit of a man's man," said Brian, poring over every curve of Jane's body, not really bothered by the cold stare coming back in his direction. Liz made introductions, Brian continued to stare, pulled himself up to his full six-foot-four-height, ran a strong hand through his flowing locks, while slightly tensing a bulging bicep, and smiled his oh so winning smile.

Jane mentally vomited. *Oh, here we go again*. She ignored Brian's outstretched hand, remarking that the ladies' wash facilities were not working, and brushed past Brian to her place in the lab. For the second time that day, Jane had left a man speechless and bewildered. Liz followed Jane grinning from ear to ear.

"Seriously, I love you drinks are on me tonight," Liz whispered into Jane's ear. "You are my hero."

Jane smiled and gave Liz a kiss on the cheek. "You are right cute, damn cute, but in serious need of brain removal," Jane offered. *I think I am going to like it here,* thought Jane.

Ian hadn't been introduced to Jane. This didn't bother him — he was used to it. People frequently simply forgot about Ian as he tended to blend in with the surroundings. "Oh, this is, erm, what's your name again?" had once or twice been used as way of introduction. He watched the scene, amused but unnoticed. Jane would figure in many of Ian's dreams and waking thoughts, but he knew she was out of his league. What Ian had to offer the world, however, was quiet determination. Unfortunately, no one in the world had yet to notice. That was one drawback to quiet determination — it didn't proclaim itself. Ian felt most at home (and usually at home in the basement) with computer games. Unlike real life, one could "power up," "equip," "evolve," and "level up" one's inanimate and super masculine alter-ego. Ian was Firelord#1. The name of his favorite game and his quiet determination to be number one formed his gamertag.[1] The bland and

---

[1] Gamertag — A gamertag is your alter ego in the gaming world. It's made from an alias, an optional avatar or picture (called a gamerpic), and a bit of info to represent you when

insignificant Ian in person was nationally known as the all-powerful Firelord #1. His weaponry was more advanced than anyone else and gamers all over the world wanted him on their team. A far cry from school days when Ian was one of the last few picked on sports teams. One of these days, the likes of Jane and Brian would notice him. He just needed "it" — *what the fuck is "it?"* Ian thought, allowing himself an infrequent f-bomb.

---

you're playing games and sharing with other people in the gaming community

IT

"Professor Knox-san, this is what we have been looking for. This is it."

Roy was still reeling from the incident with that cute little bitch. She had belittled him. He only just realized this. *Fuck*. Maybe he would take up that offer of listening to her ideas. Maybe he would suggest meeting off-site at a bar, maybe he would drop one of those pills in her drink like he sometimes did with the college girls and offer to drive her home. Maybe when she woke up sore in every orifice, she would be sorry that she messed with the great Roy Knox! Maybe... he would.

"Professor Knox-san, this is what we have been looking for! This is it!" exclaimed Tang again. "What do you think?"

Roy was now acutely aware that Tang was talking to him and he had an erection. Shifting uncomfortably in this seat (these pants must have shrunk in the wash), Roy's antennae for a good idea suddenly turned on. Erection dissipating — blood needed for the brain — Roy said, "Tang take me through that again please."

Tang was rather surprised at his mentor using the word "please." Roy was not someone to ask nicely/

Indeed the only other time Roy had used this word with Tang was during that unfortunate drunken incident at the conference. Tang blushed and repeated the findings.

"One of the biggest problems in drug discovery is getting the drug to the required site of action while not interacting and disturbing other sites in the body. Agree, Professor Knox-san?"

"Yes, get on with it!" said Roy irritably.

"With our clathrate delivery system, we can deliver any drug to any part of the body and activate it there. [2] This new clathrate even penetrates the blood brain barrier so we can even get drugs into the brain. [3] The clathrate/drug combination is inactive until the bonds are broken by a low-power laser such as this." Tang held up something resembling a large laser pointer.

Looks like a dildo, thought Roy and started imaging inserted it into Jane when he stopped himself. Roy had an uncanny knack of knowing when he was onto something — or when someone else was.

---

[2] A compound in which molecules of one component are physically trapped within the crystal structure of another.
[3] The blood—brain barrier is a highly selective semipermeable membrane barrier that separates the circulating blood of the body from the brain. The blood—brain barrier is formed by brain endothelial cells and it allows the passage of water, some gases, and molecules that are crucial to neural function. However, it is very difficult to design drugs that cross this membrane.

Tang continued to explain. "The clathrate/drug construct is lipophilic, so it easily crosses cell and blood brain barrier. Ian, one of our techs, noticed that these constructs would deconstruct under a laser wavelength of 10,600 nanometers, commonly used by surgical lasers, however, we used much lower power so the surrounding tissue is not affected."

Interesting, thought Roy, wondering who Ian was. Maybe he was that chubby kid with the bad haircut.

"Ian pioneered this work and has built this device." Tang held up the laser and admired it.

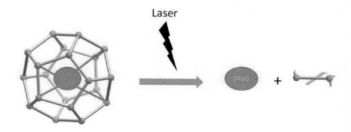

"Really remarkable!" exclaimed Tang, who was unusually animated.

The impact of these fledgling results was immediately apparent to Roy. He knew that he must quickly ask a few questions, make some banal suggestions so he could legitimately claim he was part of the process and make this his own. "Who did this work, this Ian? Which one is he?" All inventions by "his people" naturally were property of the company. The company was Knox Pharma, thereby Roy's property.

Nevertheless, Roy's ego was such that he had to own something like this in its entirety. It was already his brainchild. "Have this kid come to my office this afternoon," was all Roy said, exiting Tang's office with a spring in his step. Roy knew something big when he saw it, and this was big. This was it.

The Knox Way

The path was well trodden and clear for Roy. Cajole, caress, captivate, and claim. A winning formula and a hallmark of the Knox way. Ian was surprised when Tang informed him of his summons. Tang, although Ian's supervisor, had known Roy long enough not to try and piggyback on the meeting. He knew that this was big and he also knew that riding in Roy's wake was way better than getting in his way. Tang did not like conflict.

Ian had only been summoned to the boss's office once before. They had needed someone to hold a portrait of Roy in position while he decided upon the best place for it.

"Come in, my boy," bellowed Roy, coming from around his desk with outstretched hand. Ian had the feeling that Roy was enormous in this room. The optical illusion created by the sloping floor always worked wonders, Roy knew.

Ian, always the quiet sort, was feeling cowed *What would Firelord #1 do?* he thought. *I don't have a laser cannon or dragon scale armor here though... .*

Roy came upon him like a predator came on to prey. "You know, I always thought you had that special spark in you, my boy."

Ian hated being referred to as "my boy" but was way too scared to say so.

"This idea of yours has it flaws, serious flaws, mind you, but I think I can help you." Over the next hour Roy's bullied, bribed, and bamboozled Ian into submission. Roy's idea (yes, it was his) used Ian's original flawed idea imbibed with Roy's flair for the spectacular and they were going to be a winning team. In reality, it was a team of one and the idea had not really changed, but Ian did not work that out until much later. Ian left Roy's office with his head swimming, probably a combination of the intricate discussions and the powerful aroma of Roy's aftershave. He also felt a little nauseous. This was quite common for anyone leaving a one-on-one meeting with Roy.

Roy leaned back in his expensive leather chair. His mind was racing, so many plans to make. Wow, this was good. This was what he lived for, this was true excitement. He punched the intercom. "Mary, no calls, no one enters, I need to think." He didn't wait for a reply.

First things first, he thought, *cleanse the mind, relax, and then make plans on a clean canvas*. There was only one tried and tested method for Roy to achieve this. He unzipped his pants and started to masturbate, thoughts of where he would insert the laser into Jane "cocky bitch" Porrima on his mind. By the time he was washing his hands in his personal bathroom, plans were starting to solidify.

Ramping Up

Knox Pharma went into overdrive. Invention patents were applied for (all in Roy's name of course) and preclinical testing started in earnest. [4] Roy was at his most charismatic and implored the relatively small workforce to "go the extra mile" and "pull out all the stops." Ian received a promotion. Roy had to do something for him. However, Ian had no time to enjoy it or the extra money as he was working seven days a week. Roy had set almost impossible timelines for the Knox staff, insisted they stick to them, then gone flying around the world proclaiming the enormous impact of his discovery.

During this time, Jane felt as though she had stepped into a whirlwind. What was meant to be a chance for her to learn and hone her skills as an independent scientist and prove her parents wrong, morphed into a fly by the seat of pants, learn on the fly, why are there only twenty-four hours in a day initiation. Energized by a lifetime of being judged on her looks, she threw herself into work and realized that not only did she love it, she was good at it. Someone had to make

---

[4] Testing phase in animals before the clinical testing phase in humans

decisions on a day-to-day basis and organize the huge amount of work necessary in the most expedient fashion to achieve the timelines. In other words, she was a bitch with a whip and knew how to use it! She gained respect from all her peers with her work ethic and willingness to do any job to get "it done." She was having the best, if most exhausting, time of her life. Indeed, she couldn't remember the last time someone had peered down her cleavage or accidently brushed up against her perfectly formed butt. Not having time to shower or work out might have impacted this, but the whole group had ramped up their workload and the fervor became infectious. This was one rollercoaster they all wanted to ride.

Even Brian, who usually coasted through life like a California surfer dude, got caught up in the mayhem. He had become accustomed and even rather enjoyed being told what to do by Jane. "Yes Jane" and "what's next, Jane?" became his mantra. Who knew a boorish serial womanizer could become a rather useful lapdog? Wonders never ceased at Knox Pharma. Jane even smiled at him once in a while; this strangely made Brian's day. He worked even harder.

Ian was the brains of the operation, poring over the scientific details of every experiment. Even in his sleep, he was designing the next study. For the first time in his life, people listened to him, noticed him and indeed even sought him out. This was rather a novelty for Ian. Now he still occasionally looked over his shoulder when someone said, "Hey, I have been looking for you," only to realize it was him they had been looking for. Quiet determination morphed into a surprisingly powerful and crystal-clear scientific doctrine for the team to follow. Without knowing it, he had become a leader, though he was way too engrossed in the task at hand to realize it.

His fellow gamers in the *Firelord* community had repeatedly contacted him asking for the return of their missing inanimate leader Firelord #1. Not knowing quite what to say, he left the gaming community with a note saying he was undergoing chemotherapy and might be back if he lived. Overweight spotty youths around the world dropped like flies due to drug and alcohol overdoses, gunshot wounds, jumping off bridges, and one young man tried to hang himself from a tree. The hanging failed but as the branch broke it hit him in the head, causing a subdural hematoma. Even this didn't kill him, and he was rushed to the nearest hospital where unfortunately he was dropped off the gurney. This didn't kill him, but an ambulance rushing in a drug overdose patient (who played *Firelord*) did. Ian not only didn't realize he was a leader — he also didn't realize he was responsible for people's deaths. These would not be the last deaths related to Ian's behavior, but he didn't know that yet.

Roy was no shirker of hard work, the only proviso being that he would benefit directly. He was also not naïve enough to think Knox Pharma could go it alone. Knox Pharma was a scientific company with a great idea and potential product to sell/partner with another larger firm capable of clinical testing in humans. He and Tang (Tang could carry the bags) flew around the world, being courted by the biggest and best large pharmaceutical companies. *This is the life*, he thought, being wined, dined and, most importantly for Roy, congratulated on his brilliance.

"I told my guys, this was going to be big, I could smell it, just believe in me, I said." Roy, of course, took the lead role and Tang, of course, took notes. The rapt attention, dropped jaws and hearty slaps on the back for Roy were like a drug. He couldn't get enough of it. However, as narcissistic as Roy was, he was also pragmatic and greedy. There were two ways to show those stuck-up bastards at U Penn that he really was the best. One was to publish amazing research in the best journals. This had to wait as he knew his team were working flat out and had no time to write, and there was no way he was going to write anything. The second was to make huge amounts of money. This was a definite near-term goal. It would also get Roger that annoying limey wanker, off his back. Roy had made the error of telling Roger about the discovery, prompting Roger to force himself into some of the business meetings. This simply would not do, as Roger, unlike Tang, would not shut up, and no one took Roy's limelight. Eventually, Roy proposed a tête-à-tête at a special location just between him and Roger. The location happened to be one of the seediest brothels in Bangkok while on a layover to Paris. Roy spiked Roger's drink with one of his favorite "roofies", and quickly dumped him. Roger woke up the next day naked, bent over a chair with a very sore bottom. Subsequently, he flew back to England very glum, in need of antibiotics and with an intense itch from his groin area.

Back on American soil, Roy and Tang met with Tommy "Teflon" Turner, the business manager for Knox. The 'Teflon" moniker was given since it didn't matter how much dirt was thrown at Tommy, none of it stuck. Indeed, Tommy had managed to get Roy off several sexual assault charges over the past few years with staff and students alike. Roy liked Tommy. "A good guy" was how Roy referred to Tommy. Roy's guile and selfishness were only matched by Tommy's slipperiness and slyness. Together they were a force to steer clear of.

Experiment

During the time Roy had been away, the Knox team had made great progress. The "great idea" that Ian had come up with and Roy now claimed and owned one hundred percent was really quite simple. There was a well-known molecule, mystillate, that if injected directly into a patient's brain, had amazing beneficial effects on symptoms of Alzheimer's disease. This had been shown many years ago. However, injecting into the brain of a person with Alzheimer's disease on a regular basis was rather impractical, as well as being rather dangerous. When ingested or even injected into the bloodstream directly, mystillate did not get into the brain. In scientific terminology, it did not penetrate the blood-brain barrier. The rather annoying enigma had frustrated scientists for years. What Ian had shown was that when mystillate was combined with clathrate to make a "caged molecule," this new drug could penetrate the brain very well. Ian compared this to a Trojan horse scenario. The caged molecule would stay there inactive until the energy from the low-power laser broke the bonds. The laser was about the size of a cigar, only slightly more powerful than a regular laser pointer. Preclinical testing had indicated that holding the laser next to the temple would release the drug and amazing beneficial effects would be seen. Animal testing had shown this combination drug was safe and worked extremely well. It was this scientific discovery that had sent Roy and Tang around the world to find partners. The scientific team — Ian, Jane, Brian and Liz — had formed a strong bond over the last few months working closely together and had deliberated, voted on, and come up with a list of five potential names for the new amazing drug. Roy had barely glanced at the list then made a unanimous decision to call the drug Knoxate, and that was that.

As they had neared the final stages of testing, Ian had become obsessed over what power the laser should have. How much was enough? What if they went too high and released too much drug, what then? The laser power that was intended to be tested in humans was ten milliwatts. When mice were subjected to ten thousand milliwatts, they tended to freeze for a period but otherwise were fine. What did this freezing mean? What if this happened in humans? What if? What if? For the few hours Ian tried to sleep, he rolled these questions over in his mind. For the hours he was awake (about twenty out of twenty-four hours), he scoured the scientific literature for an answer. There, of course, was no answer. The only way to tell was to try it in a human.

Ian, Jane and Brian sat in the conference room at Knox Pharma mulling over the question of the higher power laser in humans. Liz would have been there, but she had a hot date, and as they had been so busy for the last few months, in Liz's own words, she needed to get "fucked badly." Indeed, she exclaimed her needs rather loudly one day in the lab and this had made Ian blush.

Ian was as open minded as the next man, but Liz's often very graphic comments sometimes made him feel rather nauseous. The three of them sat looking at the little orange pills in front of them, the fruit of many months of intense work. "But what if..." started Ian, only to be cut off by Jane.

Holding her head in her hands, Jane talked to the table. "If you say that one more time, I am going to kick you in the nuts."

"But—"

Jane kicked out, narrowly missing Ian's private parts and connecting with his seat. Ian got up and started to pace. Brian just watched. He didn't engage in the more cerebral aspects of this endeavor. He was a doer. Mainly doing whatever Jane asked but on occasion taking his lead from Ian. Coming from a fairly meandering lack of direction lifestyle, these last few months had been energizing for Brian. He propelled himself from one task to the next and was happy, indeed begging, for direction, mainly from Jane. Although he did not admit it to himself, he loved it when Jane told him what to do. Early on he had made some fumbling advances towards Jane and been completely re-buffed, which was a relatively novel experience for Brian. On another occasion he came close to physical harm. He dreamed of Jane. It was not unusual for Brian to dream of a woman, especially in a sexual way. All men did, didn't they? However, his dreams with Jane were different. In the past, he was always the aggressor and the beautiful young women the object of his desires. His dreams about Jane were the reverse. She was the dominant party subjecting him to all sorts of bizarre demands and he loved it! He would never tell anyone about his dreams, but the sheer presence of Jane was intoxicating. He lived to do her bidding. *God, she is so hot*, Brian mused while catching a glimpse of Jane's bra as she kicked out at Ian. *How I would love to have that in my face*. Brian often daydreamed while Ian and Jane argued.

"Brian, Brian!" Jane was shouting at him.

Brian was suddenly aware he had a major hard-on, and quickly leaned forward, embarrassed. "What?" he stammered.

"Have any ideas…?" Jane looked at him mockingly. This look, hurt Brian. Jane was everything to him. He lived for her pleasure. Her mocking cut deep. Brian was well aware of the recurrent question of power needed for the laser and the "how high should we go" question. Ian had brought this up day after day for months. The only real answer was they would have to find out in humans. This was the dilemma. What if it was bad? Any major side effect could kill Knoxate (Ian and Jane were still fuming about the name) before it had even had a chance. If they gave their baby (as Ian liked to call it) to another company to test, others might kill it before he had a chance to modify the power settings. However, the only way was to take the risk and test it in humans. This was not under their control and drove them crazy. They all had so much invested in this, not just time and money but the intense work had made this a very personal experience for them all. Exasperated at the recurrent theme, Jane had lashed out. The first object of her ire was of course her faithful puppy Brian. "Have any ideas...?" she mocked again, turning the last word into a sneer.

Brian flushed. He was angry, ashamed, and hurt. No one talked to Brian like this. He was six foot five, two hundred and forty pounds, perfect teeth, perfect hair, and he was damn cute. No one talked to Brian like this... except Jane. His first reaction was to storm out or attack back with vulgarity... he was... he paused, erection gone, and brain suddenly engaged. Somewhat of a change in the usual blood flow for Brian. A moment of calm and clarity came over him. "So we need some idea of where to start out for our dose/power escalation studies?" [5] Brian said, almost absentmindedly.

"Duh!" shot back Jane, growing angrier by the second.

---

[5] Dose escalation studies in clinical trials start with low doses of drug and methodically increase the dose until side effects are seen. The dose at which side-effects are seen acts as an upper dose limit and safety window.

"Then I will do it," said Brian in a confident authoritative tone that surprised even him. "We've done all the safety experiments we can in animals, it is safe, but we need to know what this freezing is, yes?" Brian carried on, emboldened by the silence of the other two. "We have the drug, we have the laser, let's test it on me, low power first, then high power." Brian had stood up, drawing himself to his full height. The mocking expression had gone from Jane's face.

Ian broke the silence. "That's a stupid idea," said Ian, drawing himself up to his full height of five foot six, then sitting back down.

"Why?" retorted Brian. "You told us that initial trials will most likely be in healthy young males."[6] He continued loving the adoring look (was it adoring?) that Jane was giving him. "I am a healthy young male, we need an answer, let's do this, now!" said Brian, slamming his fist down on the table. Unfortunately, Brian was as strong as he looked, the table jumped, and Ian's half-drunk cup of coffee landed in his lap.

Ian wiping himself off with a "Damn it," said, "One, it's illegal, two, it's just plain dangerous, and three, it is…"

"Thinking out of the box," cut in Jane. "I like it, it is what we need. Brian, I applaud you."

---

[6] The preferred test subject in clinical trials is a healthy young male. Most resilient to side effects and most in need of beer money.

Brian sat down, not only surprised at the turn in Jane's mood but he also got an almost instantaneous erection and the diversion of blood flow made him feel light headed.

"Brian is right," she continued. "Illegal — yes, not professional — yes, but dangerous? We know everything about this drug. Brian, I agree with you." Brian almost stained his boxer shorts.

"Whoa, hold on," said Ian. Jane and Ian argued back and forth about the pros and cons of Brian's proposal. Brian fell silent. He did not have the intellectual capacity of Jane or Ian so was way out of his depth, but he was a man of action. Without being noticed, he walked out of the conference room and made his way to the lab. As it was after hours, the lab was empty. Brian got what he needed, did what he needed to do and started a timer on his phone. Feeling calm and at peace with himself, he walked slowly back to the conference room. As expected, Jane and Ian were still arguing and barely noticed him re- enter the room.

"Ian, this is only for us to know, only to help the clinical studies. Ian, I think… . Why did you bring that in?" Jane was in full force, fired up and looking like sex on wheels. She eyed Brian quizzically. Ian pulled his hands from his greasy hair and also looked at Brian quizzically. Though he didn't look like sex on wheels, more like bland on skateboard.

Composed and somewhat straining to keep it together, Brian replied, turning his phone around to show the timer. "I just took thirty milligrams of Knoxate. In seven minutes, it should be at full effect" He pushed the cigar-shaped laser towards Jane. "Let's do this."

Ian, jaw dropped, was silent. Jane simply replied, "I love you... but not like that," she quickly retorted to Brian's expectant stare.

Brian didn't mind. She was smiling at him and that was enough. *What is happening to me?* he thought.

Ian regained his composure. "How do you feel?"

"Fine, and my pulse hasn't changed." Brian pointed at his Fitbit watch. "I am recording this.

"No side effects. I feel nothing. Turn on the laser" Brian continued. Jane moved towards the laser.

Ian quickly grabbed it. "Wait, if we do this, I am the scientific director, it is going to be my way." Jane was taken aback by Ian's dominant tone, so unlike him. She considered arguing but let it go. Ian stood up and paced, his crumpled chinos still showing the coffee stain on his groin.

"Really..." He looked at Brian. Jane looked at Ian, then at Brian. Ian had an intense look about him.

"Jane, go get the first aid kit."

Jane obeyed. Jane wondered what a Band-aid would do in this situation, but she didn't say anything. Ian focused himself on the timer on Brian's phone. Three minutes to go. Jane returned with one minute twenty-three seconds to go, looking flushed and excited.

"Okay, low power for two seconds, no more." Ian tried to say the words confidently like a man in charge, but they came out more like a whine.

"Okay," said Jane intently staring at Brian.

"Mmhh okay." Brian found it hard to concentrate under Jane's intense scrutiny. Thirty seconds to go.

"Sit down," said Jane. Brian complied,

"Yes, sit down," said Ian, after Brian had already sat down. Ian moved towards Brian with the laser. "Low power, two seconds," he said. Five seconds. Three, two, one...

"Just fucking do it!" said Jane, making everyone jump.

Low Power

Ian hit the button on the laser that was set to lower power for two seconds, then just stared. Jane stared. Brian stared back. Ian needed to pee. Brian felt nothing. Ian and Jane kept staring. Nothing. Over the next few minutes, Ian and Jane took Brian's pulse, blood pressure and in fact any measurement they could think of. Nothing remarkable.

"You know, mystillate would only show improvement cognition, memory intellect, et cetera in people who are impaired," Ian mused.

Well, Brian is as dumb as an ox, Jane mused internally.

Brian spoke up. "Our data would suggest that the peak effect should occur in less than a minute and last for a few hours. We should be at peak now. I suggest we keep monitoring for another hour, try increased times up to ten seconds over the next few days and then progress to high power... Oh and next time we should also get a reading at baseline before we use the laser, agree?" Brian didn't wait for an answer. He simply walked out to go to the bathroom. He felt fine, rather clear headed, in fact. Ian and Jane exchanged a look.

Jane pondered, *That's the most logical thing Brian has ever said*, but then thought, *Nah, can't be.*

Jose always made his rounds after normal business hours; security was, after all, his responsibility. Roy Knox had drilled that into Jose on his interview then had promptly ceased to notice that Jose existed. Indeed, Jose had found he had a knack of not being noticed. Over the last few months, Jose had quietly absorbed all the excitement around him. He loved his job and felt very protective of the company. Without being noticed, he made a note in his log using his favorite Parker pen and disappeared back into the shadows.

High Power

Over the next few days, Ian and Jane experimented with different times of low power laser values, and made many readings and recording from Brian. Most of this work was done late after everyone else was gone. Enjoying the attention and really feeling like he was part of something, Brian complied with everything. They had decided not to tell Liz, as they all knew that if anything of this got out, they could be looking at prison sentences. Liz was a great person but had a big mouth and very few filters.

"Well?" said Ian looking at Jane. She inclined her head and looked thoughtfully at Brian.

Brian imagined her on top of him naked with the same expression. *Shit*. He was starting to get hard again. Quickly he thought of Hilary Clinton and things subsided.

"Well?" Jane said.

"Let's do it," said Brian confidently, now trying to get an image of a naked Hilary Clinton out of his head.

The three of them now had the procedure down. Jane took measurements, Ian recorded the measurements and Brian sat there contented to be in

Jane's presence. "Okay, high power, two seconds." Ian's voice had just a slight quiver to it.

"Let's do it," said Brian. According to Ian, high power was a different beast. Yes, it released more of the drug, but it also went deeper into the brain and so engaged more areas of the brain than the lower power setting. Ian had warned the effects of the high-power setting could be quite different.

"Sit down," said Jane. Brian complied.

"Yes, sit down," said Ian, after Brian had already sat down. Ian moved towards Brian with the laser. "High power, two seconds," he said. Five seconds. Three, two, one… Ian hit the button.

Brian froze — no speech, no movement, no nothing. The only thing was that a slightly inane grin appeared on his face.

"Oh shit," said Jane.

"Oh no," said Ian.

"Brian, talk to me!" Jane cried. Brian's heart rate and blood pressure didn't change. Indeed, none of his physiological functions seemed affected at all. Though he did feel a little blank… Slowly he became aware of someone talking to him. "Brian, talk to me!" Jane had gripped Brian's shoulders and was shaking him.

Quite calmly, he replied, "What would you like me to say?" Jane stood back. Brian had only been out for a few seconds, but it had seemed an eternity.

A torrent of "How do you feel?" "What is your name?" "What happened?" "Are you okay?" came out of Jane and Ian.

Brian answered all questions to the best of his ability in a calm measured way. Jane and Ian started to argue about what had gone on and whether they should take Brian to the hospital. Brian sat calmly and listened. He didn't feel the urge to do anything else. Jane was stressed again and angry with Ian, as was usual. Therefore, as usual, she lashed out at Brian. "What do you think?"

"What do I think about what?" came the calm measured reply.

Infuriated, Jane picked up the cigar-shaped laser. "What did this thing do to you?"

"I don't know," said Brian in a tone that Jane felt was designed to make her angry.

"Oh, stick it up your ass." Jane stormed around the conference room, trying to think. Ian had his head bowed and was in deep thought.

"Yes, Jane," Brian said. He stood and started to remove his trousers. He then quite calmly dropped his boxer shorts, picked up the laser and started to bend over.

"What the hell are you doing?" yelled Jane. Ian raised his head and was equally shocked at the image of Brian about to insert the laser into his anus.

"You told me to stick it in my ass," replied Brian, again quite calmly, and started to insert the laser, only stopping when Jane said, "Stop!"

"Yes, Jane." Brian paused. About an inch of the laser had been inserted into his anus. He waited expectantly for his next command. Jane simply stared at him.

"Take it out and put your clothes back on," Jane said in a quavering voice.

"Yes, Jane." Brian calmly complied.

"What are you doing?" said Jane, looking perplexed at Brian.

"I am doing as you tell me," replied Brian.

Over the next few minutes Jane and Ian made and recorded measurements. Brian seemed to be fine, very calm in fact. After the freezing experience, Brian had seemed to happily comply with everything Ian or Jane said in a bizarrely literal fashion. He would do anything. Jane and Ian had to be very careful what they said.

At one point, Ian, who was exasperated out of fear of what they had done to Brian, had said, "Oh, fuck me." Brian took this literally and tried to comply with Ian's request. Brian was very strong and had started to take Ian's pants off and bend him over the table. Ian was so scared he had gone mute. Brian had Ian bent over the conference room table and had almost inserted the laser in Ian's anus, when Jane came back in and told him to stop.

"Yes, Jane." Brian stopped. Through the whole time, he had a really inane calm smile.

Jane yelled, "Put your clothes on and sit down."

Brian complied with a "Yes, Jane."

Ian, who felt like he had been raped, went to the bathroom and cried.

This is insane, thought Jane. *What have we done?* She cleaned the cigar-shaped laser off with an antibacterial wipe.

Over the next hour or so, Brian seemed to become himself again and after two hours, he was apparently back to normal. "Brian, jump up and down," Jane tested.

"Why?" replied Brian, looking perplexed. Then, looking Jane up and down while smirking he said, "Why don't you jump up and down?" he said, raising his eyebrows in anticipation.

"Go fuck yourself," said Jane, thinking that Brian was definitely back to normal.

Ian and Jane quizzed Brian for another hour, and it was clear that not only was he back to normal, he had no idea what had happened after the freezing episode. There seemed to be a blank period in his memory of a few hours. Brian remembered nothing. The bending Ian over the table episode was not brought up, too painful a memory for Ian. Indeed, Jane thought that incident should remain buried forever. One thing that had stuck in Jane's head, though, was the sight of a naked Brian. He was indeed an Adonis, perfectly muscled, and taut and... and a tripod. Jane was a heterosexual (and very attractive) woman who had seen her fair share of naked men. She liked a well-muscled man and liked a penis more for what it could do rather than the aesthetic value. However, Brian was well built in every respect. His erect penis, was really quite something, the biggest she had ever seen. No wonder Ian had been so scared. A naked erect Brian must be quite scary to a heterosexual man. However, Jane found herself getting quite turned on at the thought of a naked Brian.

What a shame this was truly spoiled by a juvenile, narcissistic, big-mouthed, arrogant asshole. Sure, Jane had some respect for Brian and the work he had put in over the last few months. However, Brian's personality was everything she loathed about men and a real turn-off. *Shame I can't just have the body and that dick, without the brain and personality*, she thought. Actually for a few hours she could, couldn't she? Jane quickly dismissed this thought and drove home, tired but mind racing with many questions. Jose had heard some of the ruckus, observed, made notes with his favorite Parker pen and carried on with his duties.

The next day, Jane, Ian and Brian shut the door to the conference room. "How did you sleep?" asked Ian, keeping his distance from Brian.

"Great," said Brian.

Ian, always the more conservative thinker, suggested that they stop everything for a while. He was scared.

Jane was quiet and thoughtful. "No," she replied, staring at the desk. Over the next hour, Jane laid out her case. They had gone too far with this to stop; this was what they had all worked for. The low power seemed fine and maybe they should just stick with this power and increase duration of laser as necessary to release more drug. Ian argued but was beaten down, with a promise from Jane of no more high-power laser use.

"We should redesign the laser without the high-power button," said Ian.

Jane agreed. "How many do we have with the high-power button?"

"About fifty with many more in production, I will go change the specs now." Ian turned. "We need to destroy the ones with the high-power button."

"I'll do it." Jane jumped up without another word and left the room. Brian, not sure what to do next, simply sat there.

Jane had thought long and hard about their predicament. She surprised herself how determined she was to get this thing on the market and would stop at nothing to achieve this goal. Inside the storeroom, Jane looked at the cigar-shaped lasers with "low power" and "high power" buttons clearly marked. For reasons that she was not entirely certain of herself, she put three lasers in her pocket and took the box back to the conference room. Brian was still there. "Brian, be a sweetie and incinerate these, please." She held out the box. Brian, always happy to comply when he was called "sweetie," did as he was told. Jane went to her office and hid the lasers, still not sure why she was doing this.

Unforgivable

When Jane next entered the conference room, she was aware of a peculiar smell. She also noticed that Ian was red-faced and looking very angry. Before she could process anything else, Roy Knox swiveled around in his chair. "There she is. We have been waiting for you," said Roy, looking Jane up and down lasciviously and grinning from ear to ear. "Have some great news," said Roy, jumping up, putting his arm around Jane's shoulders and leading her to seat.

Jane's skin was crawling; being in a room with Roy was bad enough but being touched by him was repugnant. "They sold it," interjected Ian before Roy could say any more.

"We made an informed business decision." Jane hadn't seen there was another person in the room. The conference room door closed to reveal Tommy "Teflon" Turner. Tommy took every little bit of Jane in, giving Jane a stare that a python would give a mouse. He extended his hand. Jane had dealt with many sleazeballs and left his hand hanging.

"Sold what?" She turned to Ian, completely dissing Tommy. "Did what?" exclaimed Jane.

Roy and Tommy explained that they were going to sell the rights to Knoxate to Jethro Pharmaceuticals. Ian and Jane had been under the impression that they were going to partner with another company, not sell it lock stock and barrel. If Ian was annoyed, Jane was apoplectic. They had all worked so hard on this, it really had become their baby. Selling it to make a quick buck was out of the question for Ian and Jane. Brian had difficulty following the conversation but thought Jane looked magnificent. Despite the promises of really good bonuses and "we could do this all again," and "this was best for us," Ian and Jane refused to be mollified.

Roy had expected some arguments but not this kind of rage. He could of course do whatever he wanted, he ran the company, and all the intellectual property had his name on it. He was Roy Knox for god's sake. These little shits should be glad of his leadership and guidance. This deal in the making gave Roy all he wanted. He got money, yes, but really it was the prestige. Knoxate had great potential, Roy had seen that, but it would take time and lots of hard work to get a product to market. This way Roy got instant prestige, instant gratification and instant... *God, I wish this silly little bitch — cute as she is — would just shut up. Who the hell does she think she is telling me what to do?* Roy started imagining Jane naked, tied up, in no position to argue.

"Are you listening to me?" Jane was right in his face. Angry at being jolted from his reverie, Roy stood up and stormed out shouting that it was his company and he could do what he damn well pleased. Tommy ran after Roy.

"I am going to fucking kill him," yelled Jane. For the next hour or so Ian, Jane and Brian discussed the predicament. They got nowhere. Roy could do as he wanted. He had sold not only them out, but the whole company had been sold out, just to bolster the pitiful ego of fucking Roy Knox. Demoralized, angry, hurt and dejected, they left the conference room. This was unforgivable even for a prick like Roy Knox. Ian felt betrayed. He was going to resign and go somewhere else. Where he didn't know yet. He just sat in his office looking at the blank computer screen, dejected.

Brian also sat looking at his blank computer screen. He hadn't understood much of what had been said but was really sad it was over. For a short period, he had been part of something he could not describe but it had felt great. Why did this have to end? He had never really felt his life had a deep purpose other than the next party, but these last few months had given him a purpose. Brian felt a looming sadness coming on like nothing he had ever felt before.

Jane was way beyond angry but sat in her office. She decided not to let this happen. A plan started to develop in her mind. No one fucked with Jane Porrima like this. This was an unforgivable error.

Storming into his office, closely followed by Tommy, Roy screamed, "Who the fuck do they think they are?" He slammed the door and stomped around his office, like a petulant child who had been told no.

"Just fire them?" remarked Tommy. "You are the boss."

"I will," Roy shot back, but then paused. For all his faults, and Roy had way more than most, stupidity was not one of them. Ian and Jane could cause him problems. Ian was the brains, but Jane was the driving force. As much as Roy just wanted to fire them, the deal was not yet signed. He did not want to upset the apple cart. Firing his two main scientists was not a good move. Well, not yet anyway. He dismissed Tommy and sat down to think. *Divide and conquer,* he thought. If he could take that pretentious bitch Jane out first, Ian would be easy. He would offer Jane a partnership in Knox Pharma, part of the big league she obviously wanted. Jane would be promoted to the board. Then once the deal was signed, he would remove her. Roy smiled. *I am good*, he thought and picked up the phone "Dr Porrima, Jane," — Roy was in full bullshit mode — "I think we got off on the wrong foot. Why not come to my office as I have something else to discuss with you…"

Jane put the phone down, smiled, closed her eyes, and murmured, "Let's do this" to herself. She opened her eyes, looking composed and determined. Opening her drawer, she took out one of the lasers, placed it in her pocket and walked slowly to Roy's office, by way of the lab, deep in thought.

Change of Mind

Roy was at his most charming, positively gushing about the impact Jane had made towards Knoxate. He even apologized about just thrusting the sale of Knoxate on Jane without getting her counsel. Roy normally never apologized but felt this would help Jane see this his way. Indeed, Jane had seemed to soften, and he was really beginning to think his Knox charm was doing its thing again. *Time to zero in for the kill*, he thought and mentioned the promotion to the board for Jane. He explained that while Ian was a great scientific mind, Roy felt that Ian didn't quite have the business acumen of Jane. This was the reason he had not said it at the meeting earlier today. He had wanted to inform Jane of the promotion in private, so as not to hurt Ian's feelings. At this point Roy had almost put his hand on Jane's knee but resisted the urge.

Jane looked thoughtful and then her face changed, apparently having made a decision. "Let's have a drink," said Jane getting up and walking over to the drink cabinet.

Yes, got you, thought Roy, eyes glued to Jane's perfect behind. This was easier than he had thought. *I wonder if I could fuck her?* This was turning out to be a great week. A major deal for his company, well, major deal for him really and now this cute little thing seemed to be playing ball. Oh, the things he had dreamt of doing to her. He started to get an erection. Yes, this had been a great week. He would still fire her, but after he had fucked her, and let everybody know he had.

Jane had let Roy carry on talking. She just needed an opening. At one point it almost seemed that he would reach out and touch her knee, that would have been too much to handle and she would have had to break his nose. Thinking fast, she moved out of reach and saw an opening. Roy had a full liquor cabinet with a decanter of single malt whiskey on top. Jane opened the decanter and poured two glasses. One larger than the other. In the larger whiskey glass, she dropped a Knoxate pill and swirled the contents. Turning with both glasses, she noticed Roy had been eyeing her ass and was smirking. *I really hate this guy*, she thought. However, she smiled and handed Roy the larger glass. Jane tuned out Roy's gushing praise and frequent sexual innuendoes, all the time keeping an eye on her watch. The studies they had done with Brian had indicated that the optimal time after ingestion of the pill was about twenty minutes. The laser could then be used to release the active drug in the brain. Jane had filled their glasses again and was impatiently waiting, looking at her watch. She was sure Roy was going to make a pass at her and just being in the same room as him was making her nauseous. Finally, the twenty minutes were up.

"Did I show you the new prototype for the laser?" Jane inquired. Jane pulled the laser out of her pocket and then remarked how much the portrait of Roy really had captured his look. As Roy looked away, she zapped him with high power. The last thing Roy remembered was Jane's praise of his portrait, then everything simply went blank. Roy turned to look at Jane with an inane grin on his face.

Jane decided to do a test. "Roy, jump up and down," whispered Jane. Roy jumped up and down. *Good, it worked*, she thought. She had about an hour and had to work fast. Jane instructed Roy to log on to his computer and then dictated an email. In the email Roy instructed Tommy to kill the deal with Jethro Pharmaceuticals. He, Roy, had changed his mind, simple as that. The phone rang. It was Tommy.

"Put it on speakerphone. I will tell you what to say." Tommy had been quite bemused at the sudden change of heart and asked if Roy wanted to think about it. Under Jane's instruction Roy had argued his case, finally finishing by telling Tommy to just "fucking kill it" before slamming the phone down. The call with Tommy had taken some time. Jane had only about ten minutes left. She instructed Roy to close his computer and then told him to forget everything that had happened and to not leave his office for one hour after she did. Roy agreed, still wearing the inane smile.

Jane was about to leave when she had another idea. "Roy, stand up and open your legs," Jane said as she walked towards him. Jane kicked Roy very hard in the balls. Roy doubled over and fell to the ground. Amazingly, there was still somewhat of an inane smile on his face through the grimace of pain. *I have wanted to do that for some time*, Jane thought. For the first time today, she was feeling good. Turning for the door she said, "Say thank you."

"Thank you," said Roy, still writhing in pain. Jane closed the door.

Jose had been doing his rounds and just happened to be in the vicinity. Hidden by a large plant, Jose watched Jane disappear down the corridor, made a note with his Parker pen and carried on his rounds.

Jane had emailed Ian and said she thought she may have talked sense into Roy. Ian was not convinced and continued being morose. Jane, although scared at her actions, had also felt a thrill. She had taken charge and done something drastic. *I hope to god he doesn't remember anything*, she thought. At least if she got fired tomorrow, she had at least managed to kick him in the nuts.

The next day Ian burst into Jane's office, closely followed by Brian. "Knox changed his mind, did you hear? I — I... What did you say? Wow!" Ian was quite flustered but obviously elated. Brian just stood there grinning, not quite the same way he had grinned on high dose Knoxate, but grinning all the same. An image of Brian's well-muscled body and his amazingly large penis jumped quite uninvited into Jane's mind. Oh, what she could do with that. *If only...* . Jane was getting aroused, quite unlike her naturally controlled self.

"Well, what did you say?" Ian's face came into focus right in front of her, completely quashing any amorous thoughts she was engaged with.

"I appealed to Roy's pride," Jane said simply and explained that she had persuaded Roy that selling Knoxate now would be like catching a small fish. Developing Knoxate further would reap much bigger rewards not only in terms of money but also greater prestige. This had tipped the balance. Jane came very close to telling Ian the real truth, but the presence of Brian stopped her. She felt bad about keeping the truth from these two. This was strange, she reflected because she had always been quite happy to be a loner and make her own way in life. However, the experience of the three of them working so hard together over the past few months had created quite a surprising strong bond for Jane. Ian, she thought, would understand the need for such drastic measures and she felt would keep quiet, but Brian was too stupid and had a big mouth. *And dick*, she thought, immediately admonishing herself for thinking amorous thoughts when cool logic was needed. She decided that at some point she would tell Ian.

Indeed, the power of high dose Knoxate was way beyond what she had done to that prick Roy Knox. This fact had not escaped Jane. Jane fully understood what total mind control with no memory of events meant. She had to be careful with such power, she thought to herself. The ability to change a person's views or make them do anything without any memory imprint was something that had kept her awake all night. After Jane had left Roy's office, she had felt elated at the power she had wielded. However, as she drove home, the full impact of what she had done started to sink in. Every phone call or knock at the door made Jane jump and she fully expected to see the police. Roy, she knew, would fully have no hesitation in prosecuting her. He was a mean and spiteful man. As the night wore on Jane realized that Roy had no idea of what had happened and this had turned her thoughts to the true power, she, and only she knew about. This fact was exciting and scary at the same time. She had to confide in someone and the only person she could do this to and trust was Ian. She just had to find the right time.

Roy had followed Jane's wishes and not left his office for an hour after she left. He had simply stayed where he was, on the floor clutching his balls, for sixty minutes. After which he simply got up and drove home. He woke with a hangover and really sore testicles and was not sure why. After checking his phone, he noted numerous texts and calls from Tommy as well as the folks at Jethro Pharmaceuticals. Roy being Roy, he decided to ignore them for now, and deal with them later. Wandering around his apartment, Roy pondered the evening before. He remembered having a drink with Jane in his office and then... that was it. "Wow." He thought he must have gotten really drunk. *Did I make a pass at Jane?* he thought, *and why are my balls aching so much?* As the coffee brewed, the phone rang. It was Tommy.

"I did what?" screamed Roy into the phone.

Reversal

Roy had showered and examined his swollen testicles. *I must have fallen over drunk and hit them*, he thought. He then dressed and raced into the office. Tommy was waiting for him outside his office. Inside Tommy gave him the full story of how he they had spoken on the phone and the emails Roy had written. Tang had also tagged along. He was still the head of research but often felt like a spare part. Roy didn't consult him on anything, and Ian had taken the reins of most of the scientific decisions. Tang was actually quite annoyed, which for Tang was quite unusual as he usually just went with the flow, even after that regrettable incident with Roy at the conference. Shame forced Tang to eradicate this from his mind. Roy Knox was still his mentor and he was loyal to him. Right now, though, as usual, he had no idea of what was going on. Roy also was more than a little bemused at what had happened. The "little bitch," his new moniker for Jane, had obviously got him drunk and then made suggestions to him. She had tricked him, and she would pay, oh yes, she would pay. Roy was still surprised that he remembered nothing, but his rage and vengeance were taking over. That bitch would pay. Tommy and Tang still discussed strategy about what to do. Roy had phased them out; he was forming a plan. No one messed with Roy Knox and got away with it. Roy understood people and understood what went on in the darkest parts of people's minds. He knew this because he lived there. Rather than repel the dark thoughts that existed in all of us, Roy Knox reveled in them. Roy punched the intercom. "Mary, get Holger at Jethro on the phone. Get out!" he barked at the rest. Everyone in his office scuttled away.

Roy had always won because, even though he made enemies they never knew how low he was prepared to go. He was not just prepared to go low — he started there. "Holger, how are you doing?"

Sounding rather bemused, Holger simply replied, "What the hell is going on?"

"Relax and let me explain." Roy poured himself a stiff drink and went into charm mode. "I am but a man and a man with faults and weaknesses, Holger. Man to man, let me explain." Roy explained that his staff did not want to give up Knoxate and one person in particular had made it very clear that she would do anything to change Roy's mind.

Something that only Roy knew was that the ladies changing room for the labs at Knox Pharma was fitted with a video camera. Most of the female scientists at Knox were not worth the memory card storage. However, one definitely was. One thing about being a sleazeball was that it took one to recognize one.

"Remember those pictures I showed you, of Jane…" Roy left the sentence hanging.

"Mmh, yes, maybe," Holger stuttered.

"Let me show you something." Roy initiated a video call. The next few minutes showed multiple scenes of Dr. Jane Porrima undressing. Her perfect tits and ass were on display, in multiple undressing scenes. Roy had played the video many times, usually while masturbating. Right now, he was completely flaccid. This was business. When the video finished, there was silence. *I bet he has a hard-on*, thought Roy. "Well, this is why I sent the email yesterday." Again, Roy let it hang.

"What, what has this got to do with anything?" spluttered Holger.

"This has everything do to with it." Roy started the video again. He explained that Jane was very upset at his business with Jethro. She had tricked him. Jane had come to his office, got him drunk and thrown herself at him. As Roy described the amazing sex, knowing full well that Holger was still viewing Jane's perfect naked body on the video, Holger was quiet apart from a muffled scream. *Bingo*, thought Roy.

"You see, Holger, I am but a man, what could I do?" Roy decided to deliver the killing blow. "In fact, as I was typing the email to you, she was under my desk sucking my dick. Holger, I implore you, what would you have done?" Roy thought he heard another whimper from Holger. Allowing time for Holger to clean himself up, Roy waited a few seconds.

"However, I am a man of business, Holger. I am imploring you, please forgive my weakness, come and see me, we can work something out… maybe you, Jane and I can work something out…" Again, Roy left the sentence hanging.

"What do you mean, you, Jane and I?" Holger whispered, sounding dazed.

"Come out from your high-class New York office and see how we do things in Jersey." Roy was not sure he should have hit things so head on but time was slipping away. Drastic times called for drastic measures.

"Really… you, me and… her?"

Roy smiled. He definitely knew a sleazeball when he saw one. "Come on over, we'll have a party." Roy finished the call.

"Jane! How are you? Bit of a hangover myself, wow, really tied one on last night… . Have a bit of business to discuss. Let's meet at T-Bones tonight… Great see you, then." Roy put down the phone before Jane could answer.

Roy was not sure what Jane had done to him. He assumed she had spiked his drink, but no one fucked with the great Roy Knox. He reached into his desk drawer and pulled out a small container of pills. Flunitrazepam was a benzodiazepine, better known as a "roofie." It had served Roy well in the past. As a scientist, he knew all about the enhancement of the

GABA system in the brain and the associated amnesic qualities. A number of U Penn students had fallen foul of the batch (Roy had synthesized it himself in the labs at U Penn). When given with alcohol, unknowingly spiked by Roy, the "drunk" female was led away by the chivalrous Professor Roy Knox. What happened later was only really known by Roy and the deviant recesses of his mind. The students awoke feeling hungover, often sore and completely embarrassed. The jovial, charming and gentlemanly Roy explained that he also had had a bit to drink and he really shouldn't have, but was forced by the advances of the young lady in question. The young lady, struggling to remember the night before, naked in front of a dressed Roy, reacted in one of two ways: tears or anger. As they dressed, under the intense gaze of Roy, tears were met with sympathy and hugs; anger was met with retaliation. The retaliation would be in the form of "people saw you drunk with me," "who would believe you?" and "I am a professor and could easily ruin your career."

Apart from acrimony and gossip, Roy had survived all accusations. Indeed, the vast majority of the young women simply ate their humiliation and moved away from the "great" Professor Knox. Roy neither knew nor cared what pain they went through, counselling they had to undergo or that many slumped into depression, a few even having suicidal thoughts. He neither knew nor cared.

Jane Porrima had pissed off Roy. She would learn the hard way this was a bad idea. Roy as usual had a plan — the first coercion, the second a chemically induced nightmare for Jane. The second option was drastic and dangerous, but one Roy would surely enjoy. *God, it is good to be me*, Roy thought as he leaned back in his chair, touching himself.

Jane put the phone down. Roy had not given her a chance to reply. She leaned back in her chair, eyes closed, thinking. Jane never panicked. She was always cool, calm and collected, but Roy worried her. She felt he could go places where normal people would not. She would have to be on her guard. Jane pulled out her mobile. "Got a minute?' she texted to Ian.

When Ian arrived, Jane motioned for him to close the door. "Roy wants to meet me for lunch. Did he invite you?"

"No, but I am playing golf with him at three p.m. this afternoon," Ian replied.

Divide and conquer then, but what is he up to? Jane thought. She couldn't keep using Knoxate on Roy. He would figure it out. How could she keep Roy from changing things? Should she tell Ian how she had changed Roy's mind? What was Roy up to? Questions swirled in Jane's mind.

Ian was a critical thinker; he was not as decisive and forceful as Jane but matched her in intellect. He knew something was amiss in the stories he had heard over the last twenty-four hours. The dramatic turnaround in Roy's wishes, the invite for golf — Jane was not telling him the whole story. She also looked very nervous. This was unusual for Jane. They were partners, he trusted her, and she should trust him. "What really happened last night?" Ian's gaze met Jane's. Jane first looked shocked, evasive, then she teared up. Crying was something Ian had never seen Jane do.

"I have to tell you something, but please do not interrupt until I finish." Jane collected herself wiped away a tear and began. Jane left nothing out, and Ian, as promised, did not interrupt. When she finished, there was silence. Ian explored the angles in his mind then looked up at Jane. What he said next surprised Jane. "Drastic times call for drastic measures. Damn powerful stuff, that Knoxate. We have to keep control of it no matter what." Ian spoke in a strong, calm and measured voice.

Jane expected the usually timid Ian to mince words and look on the dark side. *Wow*, she thought. *He does have steel in there*.

"But what is Knox up to?" quizzed Jane. "Why he is meeting with both of us separately? He doesn't need us. He can just change his mind again."

"I thought about that. I think he does need at least one of us" said Ian, still looking strong and in charge. Jane was impressed. "He changed his mind, well, we both know you did." Ian smiled and continued. "To change his mind again so quickly looks weak and he may change it again. Jethro Pharma may not be convinced. He needs one of us to take the fall or support him in the change back to Jethro." Ian was in full analytical mode. "It needs to look like he listened to his senior advisors and will use this to support his change of mind." Ian had gone back to his timid self "What do you think?" he finished, looking to Jane for support. "Maybe," she said. *Maybe he is just a mean bastard hellbent on revenge*, she thought.

Jane had been summoned to T-Bones, a steak restaurant for twelve-thirty. She arrived purposefully fifteen minutes late and was surprised to see Roy was not alone. Tommy "Teflon" Turner and a short fat balding man were at the table with Roy. They were looking at his phone and laughing. Roy's companions turned beet red at seeing Jane. Roy never seemed to get embarrassed at anything, but Roy did quickly put his phone away. All three men stared Jane up and down, lascivious sneers on their faces. Jane was used to being mentally undressed by men, but this was unusual that they were being so blatant about it. *Here we go, let's see what this fucker is up to*, she thought.

"You requested a meeting, Roy." Jane purposefully dropped the "Professor" and ignored the others. She was not going to be cowed by this motley crew, or any man for that matter.

"Jane, Tommy you know, of course, and this sprightly fellow is Holger Stubb, CEO of Jethro Pharma." The short fat man stood up — not a good idea as he was a lot shorter than Jane — and proffered a sweaty hand. Jane ignored him and turned to Roy.

"I was under the impression that you had changed your mind about Jethro," Jane replied.

"Well, yes but how can I say, I was coerced into it." Roy gave Jane a dramatic wink. "Come and have a drink." Roy shifted his large bulk to give Jane just enough space to sit. Although the thought of being so close to Roy or any of these vile gentlemen at the table made Jane feel nauseous, she was curious what he was up to and what was the theatrical wink all about?

Roy was directing the conversation at the table; he was a master of manipulation and deftly maneuvered conversations to suit his goals. Despite his aching balls and confusion about how he had hurt them, he was in a good mood. A glass arrived for Jane and Roy immediately played the genial host and poured Jane a glass with wine. Jane was on full alert mode and asked for a glass of water. She sipped the water, looking nonchalant, but aware of many furtive glances in her direction. Roy had many potential outcomes in mind for this meeting, none of them good for Jane.

After maneuvering the table through small talk, the jovial Roy decided it was time to get to business. Jane had not touched her wine, but Roy as ever had more than one plan of attack. "Gentleman, and lady, of course". Roy smiled towards Jane. "Let me get to the reason why we are here…"

Jane brought the glass of wine to her lips. Roy's eyes rested on Jane's glass just a fraction too long. *Interesting*, she thought and took a mouthful of wine as Roy paused.

Roy had several potential outcomes for this meeting. One was taking Jane to a local motel and all three of the guys fucking her brains out. Shortly before Jane arrived Roy had shown still pictures of Jane's naked body to Tommy and Holger. He had also said that when Jane drank, she got randy and was insatiable. He had told the guys that Jane had come to his office and seduced him over a bottle of wine to change his mind. "Maybe we could all have a little fun after lunch, if we are lucky, eh?" Roy had the guys at the table baying and salivating with lust as Jane arrived. Sex with Jane would be fun, Roy thought, but taking pictures of Jane with the guys would give him power over Jane for a long time. He could destroy her whenever he wanted. These thoughts momentarily paralyzed Roy. He had paused in mid-sentence. Quickly he reset and started again "the reason why we are here is…"

Jane had said nothing. She brought the glass of water to her mouth and slowly spat the wine into the water glass. She repeated this process a few more times as Roy waffled on, the mixture of the pale chardonnay and water barely noticeable. This hardly mattered as the focus of the table was mostly on Jane's breasts. Roy, again playing the genial host, refilled Jane's glass. The mood of the table was ebullient and excited. However, with this excitement, Jane felt a sinister undertone. The smell of testosterone was almost noticeable. This nauseated Jane, but she was still curious of what Roy was up to. She was also a little frightened. These guys had a wild look in their eyes, and Roy had seemed to garner these pathetic guys into some sort of frenzy. Jane had had to use her black belt skills on a few occasions as guys had tried to take advantage. She had even left a few with broken bones. However, these guys were hunting as a pack, and at their lead was a devious wolf. As the waiter walked by, Jane indicated there was a fly in the water glass and requested a clean one. The wine and water mixture had started to fill the water glass. She needed to get rid of it. As the full glass of wine and water were removed, Jane had stretched slightly, pushing her chest forward. They didn't notice a thing. *Idiots*, Jane thought taking a large swig of fresh water; she needed space in the glass.

Roy had moved the conversation to the afternoon she had come to his office. Jane wondered what Roy knew or suspected. She took a large swig of wine. Roy again paused, eyeing the glass of wine. *You devious fucker*, she thought.

Roy then started to describe how Jane had seduced Roy in a ploy to change his mind. Jane was stunned and for a moment dumbfounded. How could anyone believe such a ridiculous and disgusting story? Was this all Roy had? Jane simply stared at Roy. To her horror, she had started to blush and had yet to reply. Roy had started to describe the events in quite a graphic manner. Jane was simply staring at Roy, aware that the rest of the table were staring at Jane, mentally undressing her and God knew what.

Oh my god, they believe him, Jane thought as she surveyed the table. She was incredulous with disbelief. Roy continued, clearly enjoying himself, making the case that, although he had thought with his dick, the brain had taken over and was asking Holger to forgive him and re-start the collaboration. Holger was sweating profusely and breathing hard. He was also barely trying to conceal his fixation with Jane's cleavage. Jane had had enough. Even if these loathsome creatures had been taken in by Roy, no one in their right minds would be, would they?

"What the fuck! What a pile of garbage! That never happened, Roy! That's a lie! Bunch of fucking lies!" Jane's voice had risen higher than she had wanted. She was also now fully red in the face, but she had to stop this madness. Jane had risen to her feet, speaking in a calmer but threatening voice. "I do not know what you are up to, Roy, but I have witnesses to your disgusting lies. You will be hearing from my lawyer."

"Lies, you say." Roy was quite composed, unnervingly so for Jane. "Then how do I know about the heart-shaped mole under your left breast, about here, I seem to remember??" Roy pointed towards Jane's left breast. Jane's breasts had been the recipient of many stares from the table. Now she felt like a piece of meat being thrown to the wolves. Roy continued, "And you have a small scar here, appendix, was it?" pointing towards Jane's groin, his finger perilously and purposefully close to Jane's groin. Jane's business suit pants and the "v" between her thighs were now the focus of the table. Tommy involuntarily licked his lips.

How the hell did Roy know this? How did he know about the mole and her appendix scar, how… ? Jane did something she very rarely did. She started to cry. The knowledge that Roy had somehow seen her naked and described it to these loathsome guys at the table had caught her by surprise. The ridiculous story of her seducing Roy she could have dealt with, but how did he know?

Roy knew he had scored a point. Just a small amount of doubt was enough to support any incredulous story, especially when sex was involved. Roy had played this game many times before and always won. Jane was red faced, tearing up, and obviously wondering how he knew these things about her body. Having executed the first phase of his plan, he now went for the cherry on the cake. "Jane, I appreciate you may be upset, you have reason, but you did throw yourself at me, what could I do? Let's you and I go for a drive and work things out." Roy was smiling and looking fatherly at Jane. He had given her enough drug in the first glass of wine. She was not looking drunk, but it should start working soon. *This is going to be a great day after all,* he thought. Tommy and Holger just stared wide-eyed at Jane. Roy cocked his head, looked Jane in the eyed and smirked. Jane was surprised how vulnerable she felt and disgusted in herself for crying. Before she knew it, she had told the table to fuck off and run out of the restaurant crying. Jeers, laughter, and "come back" had followed her.

That's a shame, thought Roy. *I could have had some fun with her, despite my aching balls. Oh well never mind, I got my main goal, now let's work on the other one.* Roy had figured that he could move Holger and Jethro back to the negotiating table with the fabricated Jane story. Holger, Roy knew, had dark desires, and was infatuated with Jane. It took one to know one. However, the board at Jethro had been impressed with the way Ian had developed Knoxate. As much as Roy had tried to trump all of Ian's successes and make them his own, he knew that Ian's reputation had the respect of Jethro's board. Now that Jane had provided a useful reason to re-start discussions, Roy had to get Ian on his side, and he knew just how to do it. As Roy finished his wine, he smiled and thought, *God, it is good to be me!*

Jose had decided to take his lunch break out of the building. While inconspicuously sipping on ice water and eating a turkey club sandwich, he had observed the meeting. He was not a man to judge people harshly but believed people should be treated with respect, at least until reason proved otherwise. He took out his pen and made a note in his little black book and proceeded to go back to work.

Vengeance

Jane had stormed out of the restaurant incredibly mad at herself for crying, but she had been taken off-guard by the things Roy knew about her. She drove to a nearby parking lot, parked away from other cars and cried like she had not cried since she was a small girl. Once the tears were out of her system, she stared out of the windshield, thinking. Jane had grown up with everything laid out in front of her — money, looks intelligence, everything but real love. Her never-there parents had quite early in her life taught Jane to not rely on anyone, and that crying got her nowhere. As she wiped the tears away and re-applied her makeup, she went through many options. Although it was absolutely absurd and he had no way to back the story up, Roy had created enough of a smokescreen to discredit Jane and probably soon fire her, even if she did not quit out of sheer embarrassment. This she assumed had been Roy's plan. Despite the absurdity of Roy's version of events, it did appear that he had Holger and Jethro back in line for the deal. The anger welled up inside and through sheer force of will, she controlled it. Now was not the time for emotion. She needed a clear head. After giving the matter some more thought, she picked up her phone.

"Ian, we need to talk."

Jane's normal approach to life was to fight all her own fights, and for the most part she usually won. However, in this scenario, she could not see an appealing option. She needed to tell Ian what had happened, and she also needed to know what Roy's plan for Ian was. Ian, although meek, mild mannered and geeky, had struck Jane as a solid guy. He was not the kind of guy Jane had ever hung around with, but he had proven himself surprisingly well as a friend and partner in this venture.

Ian had listened without comment to what Jane had said. He was sensitive man and a small tear welled in his eyes when Jane had described the more salacious parts of the meeting with Roy. They had agreed to keep each other updated with Roy's antics and would fight him any way they could.

"What do you think he has planned for you, Ian?"

"Don't know," he replied, but blushed a little. Jane could not see him blush but heard the quaver in his voice.

"Take Brian with you."

"Why?"

"And give him Knoxate, high dose."

"What?"

Jane explained that Roy was up to something and having a compliant bodyguard that would ultimately forget everything at a later date, due to the high dose Knoxate, could be a useful thing. Ian thought for a few seconds, agreed, and quickly went to find Brian. It was two p.m. and the golf was at three. He had to move quickly.

Ian and Brian arrived at the Brinkstone Golf Club shortly before three. Brian was happy to come and play golf and even happier that Ian had brought him coffee. Ian had played golf all of three times before and looked around for the pro shop to go and get some rental clubs. He had just located the pro shop when a large hand smacked him on the back.

"There you are, my boy." Roy was beaming and pumping Ian's hand. "Thought we could just have a nice round of golf and a chat, man to man," Roy said, winking and giving Ian a knowing smile.

His smile dropped when the imposing figure of Brian ambled up. "Hi Roy, thanks for inviting me."

Roy faltered momentarily but quickly regained his composure. "Of course, no problem," he bellowed a little too loudly.

Ian observed the reaction in Roy. *This was not part of your plan, was it, Roy?* he thought, mentally thanking Jane for her foresight. Just having Brian along did give Ian some confidence. Roy went off to book another cart. Ian looked at his watch. The inactive Knoxate should be at about the right level in Brian's brain. "Have you ever used that driver?" said Ian, pointing to a large black golf driver given pride of place in the pro shop. As Brian's head turned, Ian pulled out the laser and pointed it at Brian's temple. The laser was set to high power. Brian had started to answer Ian's question, then went mute and simply stood there with an inane smile on his face.

The first two holes had gone without incidence, and to Ian's delight, Roy seemed a little miffed that Ian had shared his cart with Brian. Obviously, Roy had planned to have just the two of them in the "middle of nowhere." Ian again thanked Jane's foresight. However, he knew he had to find out what Roy was up to. Brian had won the first two holes. Any sport had always come naturally to him, and he was again first to tee off at the third hole. Despite sporting an inane grin that was really getting under Roy's skin, Brian drove the ball right down the middle of the fairway.

Roy was next. He was not playing well, and he needed to get Ian alone. His not playing well and inability to get Ian alone caused tension in his shoulders. This on top of a dull ache in his balls did not combine to give a good swing. Roy's almighty swing had sent his golf ball hurtling towards a small copse of trees and almost into the lake. "Damn," he swore and stomped off to his cart.

Ian had never been a sportsman and golf was not an exception to this rule. However, he was a critical thinker and knew he needed to get some alone time with him to Roy. Ian aimed towards the copse of trees and gave the club a lazy swing. Ian had worked out that if he didn't try to hit the ball too hard, the ball went roughly in the direction he wanted. It might take him many shots to reach the others, but he didn't really care. This was not about golf and the two of them knew it. Brian thought it was all about golf and was clearly having a great time as he was grinning from ear to ear.

Sure enough, Ian's ball went in the direction of the trees. Not as far as Roy's, but Ian was quite pleased with himself. "I will come with you, Roy, our balls have gone in the same direction," Ian hollered after Roy. Roy looked pleased. As Ian pulled a nine iron out of his bag, he told Brian to take his second shot and then come back for them.

"Yes, Ian," Brian said, smiling. Ian only wanted to give Roy a small period of time. Roy scared Ian and he didn't want to be left alone too long with him.

Roy drove the two of them off toward Ian's ball. This was his chance and Roy moved in fast. Roy immediately quizzed Ian on his thoughts regarding Jethro and was not happy to hear Ian was against it. Ian took another two shots to get near Roy's ball near the copse of trees. He could tell Roy was getting irritated and really wanted the Jethro deal. What he didn't understand was why he needed Ian to be on board. Roy was after all the boss. He could make a unilateral decision.

Roy was not a man who was beaten easily; he would stop at nothing to get his goal. He thought there was a chance he could pull the Jethro board around without Ian's support but knew it would be much easier with him. Time to play dirty. Roy pulled out his phone. Ian, sensing danger, wondered where Brian had got to.

In fact, Brian was way ahead of the other two. His second shot of the par five had landed just short of the green and he was now on his way back.

Roy Knox was a man with a plan, and a backup plan — he thought ahead. Tommy "Teflon" Turner had been his faithful associate for many years. Tommy did things without question and had no more scruples than Roy. Tommy had been asked to follow and get dirt on almost everyone Roy had worked with in the last ten years. Often Tommy came up with little but occasionally he uncovered a diamond, and Roy pocketed this diamond for potential later use. On one of the times Tommy had followed Ian, Tommy had a natural ability to lurk unseen, and the information passed back to Roy had provoked an arching of the eyebrows. These pictures were now on the phone being shown to Ian.

Ian just started. He was speechless and humiliated. Not sure of his own sexuality, Ian had explored relationships with women and men. Being a critical thinker, he had made this a very pragmatic endeavor. As he wasn't the most attractive, outgoing or gregarious of men, relationships with either sex had been few and far between. As a scientist, Ian knew that a proper scientific conclusion often required multiple observations. The only way for Ian to "sample the population," as he thought of it, was to pay for prostitutes. He was also a very private person and so went to great pains to keep his "exploration of self" exactly that. Usually, he went to the big cities of New York and Philadelphia where anonymity was easier. However, Ian had also been corresponding online with people of like-mindedness, under a pseudonym of course. An offer to meet face to face quite nearby had surfaced and quite uncharacteristically for Ian, he accepted. Justin, who had invited Ian for a face to face, had seemed very warm and genuine online. However, face to face Justin had apparently forgotten to mention his extensive tattoos and multiple piercings as well as his penchant for illegal drugs. In addition, he had been very aggressive and tried to hustle Ian for money.

Tommy had not been "on duty" that night but made a habit of hanging around sleazy bars, when the obviously out of place Ian had walked in. Not a man to look twice at a gift, Tommy had followed the two men. Justin had made a number of crude moves and suggestions, before Ian had politely excused himself to go to the bathroom and made a run for it. The episode had been confined to history and Ian had been way more careful about his online persona ever since. Tommy had struck up a conversation with Justin and quite quickly learnt of his penchant for bondage and sadomasochism. He even gave Tommy that web address of his pay per play show. Still shots from the explicit leather-clad antics of Justin, along with photographs of Ian and Justin in a passionate embrace were now showing on Roy's screen. Ian simply stared at the screen, his eyes slightly glassy.

Roy put a fatherly arm around Ian. "Look, my boy, no hard feelings, but I need your support. Give me your support with the Jethro folks and we will delete these together." Roy could see how upset Ian was, and knew this was a key moment. Roy knew about unhappiness, and what a motivator it was. He was a master of dealing it out. No matter what, Roy Knox always got his way.

Without a word, Ian shrugged of Roy's embrace and walked towards his ball. Being gay was not a crime or something to be ashamed of, Ian knew that, but the horrid pictures of Justin in positions that Ian never knew existed alongside the intimate images of Ian and Justin told an untrue story, but one that could be believed. Some men would have laughed it off and called Roy's bluff, however, Ian was a very private and sensitive person. The very thought of people talking about him in this way made Ian nauseous. Ian was not the sort of person to be in a scandal. At this moment in time, even his normally logical and pragmatic approach to life offered no options. He was scared and humiliated.

To say Brian was having a great time would be hard to say. The high dose Knoxate had put his brain on autopilot. He functioned robotically and commands or requests that were made of him simply seemed to be a good idea. Indeed, one could compare the effects of high dose Knoxate to hypnosis in a way. The internal thoughts and reactions were temporarily shelved in favor of an external command. The third hole was a par five dogleg left. Brian had driven his tee shot almost three hundred yards straight down the fairway to the elbow of the fairway. This opened up a view of the hole and Brian had hit a five iron to the edge of the green. Brian had simply followed Ian's commands, had executed the two shots perfectly, all with inane grin, of course and was now approaching Roy and Ian.

Roy had wanted more time with Ian but at least he had got his point over. As he walked by Ian, he conspiratorially whispered, "We can do this, my boy, you and me together."

Brian parked the golf cart next to Roy's and walked over to the two men. Eyeing his ball, Roy looked at his club. It was a nine iron. He needed a different club, and he also needed a few more seconds with Ian.

Brian strolled up with a cheery "Hi, guys" and was of course sporting an inane grin.

Roy thought Brian had been drinking or smoking something. The inane grin was getting on his nerves. "Brian, can you get me a five iron, please?" Turning to Ian, he said, "Look, Ian, when I first took you on, I realized what huge potential you have. I am your friend and really just trying to help you. I know these silly photos may seem a strange way to go about it, but I need your support and you need my guidance. We could both be famous and rich over this. You and me together, a great team, eh? What do you think?" Roy refrained from putting his arm around Ian.

Brian was strolling back with the five-iron, grinning. Turning to Ian and putting his back to Brian,

Roy said, "Come on, my boy, you know it makes sense."

Ian again said nothing. He was scared, confused and on the verge of tears.

"Here it is, Roy." Brian held out the club.

Roy, with his back to Brian, whispered, "Please, Ian, you know it makes sense. Don't play hard ball with me."

The words escaped Ian's mouth before he had really thought about them. "I wish you were dead, Roy!" The tears now came uncontrollably. Ian turned sank to his knees and wept. He didn't know what else to do.

Brian had been unable to hear what the two men had been talking about on his approach. However, he did hear the exclamation from Ian. To his Knoxate-controlled brain, this seemed a good idea. He swung the club. Brian was a good golfer with a great swing. He was also powerfully built. The head of the five-iron caught Roy just behind the ear, crushing that area of skull and breaking the club in two. Roy fell face down, killed instantly, though Brian was not to know that. Brian was now left holding the severed shaft of the club. For a moment he looked at the broken club, then with considerable force, he rammed the shaft of the club through Roy's back, piercing his heart and lungs and pinning Roy to the ground.

Ian stopped sobbing when he turned to see what the noise was. "What the fuck did you do?"

Grinning widely and quite nonchalantly, Brian said, "You wanted him dead, you wished it."

"Oh no," exclaimed Ian, looking around as his brain went into overdrive. Luckily, this part of the course was quite secluded. However, players could be along soon. "Brian, take the body to the trees over there."

Quite happily, Brian obeyed, Roy Knox was a big man and even Brian with his massive physique had some trouble pulling Roy's corpse over to the trees, but he managed it. Ian looked at his watch. He was now in full logic mode. He calculated that he had about twenty minutes left of Knoxate in Brian's system. Ian took Roy's phone and wallet. The phone was locked. However, Ian had noticed that Roy had used his thumbprint to unlock the phone. Bending over Roy, Ian took Roy's hand and opened the phone, Ian then quickly reset the access settings and asked Brian to cover the body with brush. Ian took the head of the broken club and threw it into the lake, the shaft of the club was still inserted into Roy, he would have to deal with that later. He then instructed Brian to wash the blood off his arms in the lake, drive one of the golf carts back to the clubhouse, and take Roy's car and drive to Knox Pharma. Once there, he was to go to the storeroom and go to sleep. Once back in his car, Ian drove to a nearby parking lot, strangely enough the same one Jane had gone to after her encounter with Roy, and opened the phone. Roy's phone proved to be a treasure trove of information about just how devious and sordid a guy Roy was. It also gave Ian access to almost every part of Roy's digital life — password, accounts, email, texts everything. After about thirty minutes, he closed Roy's phone, opened his phone and called Jane.

Cover Up

Jane and Ian were sitting in the storeroom at Knox Pharma looking through Roy's phone. Jane agreed with Ian that the phone could prove very useful in the long-term. However, they were both fixated on the short-term issue — namely, what to do with Roy's body. Brian was asleep in the corner snoring loudly. As it was after hours, there was nobody in the building. At least, this was what they thought. After a series of "you did what," "oh my god" and "oh fucks," Jane had calmed down and agreed with Ian that they both needed to "chill and think straight." Although very different in personality and their approach to problems, Jane and Ian worked very well together. Both were critical thinkers and excelled at difficult problems. Jane had the wild, lateral thinking, crazy ideas that might just work, and Ian modified the idea so that it could work.

A little after eight p.m., they had a plan and woke Brian. The story was that Brian had got drunk on the golf course and Ian had brought him here to sober up. Brian said he did not remember a thing. Ian and Jane exchanged glances and smiled. Any memory of what had just happened from Brian would scupper the whole plan.

"I don't feel hungover, though, that's weird." Brian was completely confused and looked between Jane and Ian.

"Probably still drunk. You must be thirsty. Here, drink this." Jane had produced a glass of water and Brian, always happy when Jane asked him to do anything, drank it. "I will drive you, Brian," she said rising to her feet.

Although his mind was still swimming with what had happened and he was really quite worried that he had no recollection of the golf game, apart from arriving there, he gladly accepted Jane's offer. Ian nodded to Jane as she left the conference room. Ian went back to studying the phone. They had agreed that their plan could be split into two parts — the short-term plan, getting rid of Roy's body — and the long-term plan, pretending to be Roy Knox.

Short-Term Plan

Brian was having a great time. He just loved being in Jane's presence. There was something about her he couldn't put into words. When they first met, Brian had approached Jane, figuring his looks and physique would open the door (and legs) as they usually did. However, Jane had re-buffed him quite strongly and he had given up. Plenty more fish in the sea was his motto. However, the intensity of this Knoxate project had brought them working closely together over an extended period of time. He had a longing for Jane that went way beyond mere sexual desire. He was so intoxicated with Jane's presence just merely talking to her in the car was heavenly. He didn't notice nor care that Jane had gone the long way home to his house, via the golf course.

"Isn't that where you played golf, Brian?" Jane said nonchalantly. She surreptitiously took the laser out of the inside pocket of her jacket.

"Yes. Strange though, I don't remember anything about the game. I must have been really drunk. I hope Roy wasn't too angry." In anyone else's presence, his words would not have bothered Brian. However, in admitting he was drunk to Jane, he was embarrassed.

Jane felt Brian's embarrassment and realized despite his crass, "frat boy" demeanor, he did actually have a gentler and caring side to him. Admonishing herself for frivolous thoughts, Jane went back to the task at hand. "Is that the clubhouse?" Jane pointed into the distance. As Brian turned to look, Jane zapped his temple with high power. Brian didn't get to respond; he went mute for a few seconds, then a really large grin came across his face. Jane felt bad about putting Brian through another high dose of Knoxate so soon. They did not know anything about the long-term consequences of Knoxate, but desperate times called for desperate measures, to coin Ian's phrase.

Jane parked the car on a back road that skirted the golf club. Ian had given very specific directions to the body. A split rail fence denoted the boundary of the golf course. It was old and dirty, not an easy thing to tackle in a business suit. Jane looked at Brian. Brian gazed back with an inane grin.

"Pick me up and put me over the fence."

"Yes, Jane."

Brian was six foot four and powerfully built. He easily picked Jane up and walked towards the fence. Jane could feel his arm and chest muscles against her. She looked up at him, grinning. *He really is quite an attractive man,* she thought. *Shame he is such an arrogant dickhead.* Brian placed Jane gently over the fence then vaulted it effortlessly. He stood there looking at Jane, grinning. For a few seconds, Jane was having amorous thoughts and for the second time that day, she admonished herself for being weak. "Follow me."

"Yes, Jane."

Ian's directions had proved accurate and they quickly found the body, despite the cloudy night sky. Before they had woken up Brian, Ian had found some extra-large heavy-duty garbage bags. "A lab is a really great place to find all sorts of useful stuff," Ian had exclaimed. Jane instructed Brian to remove the shaft of the club from Roy's back, put one bag around his lower half and the second around his upper half. Roy had been disgusting in life. In death he was even worse. Rigor mortis had set in, and the placing of Roy in the garbage bags was causing Brian much exertion. However, he happily complied with Jane's request, grinning all the way.

To take her mind of the grotesque image of Roy's face, Jane focused her gaze on Brian. His biceps were bulging and sweat was starting to appear on his brow. Brian usually wore shirts to show off his physique and today was no exception. Jane could clearly see his back muscles working hard to coerce the now stiff Roy Knox into the bags. One of Roy's hands split the side of the bag. Jane and Ian had thought of this. As Brian held, pushing with all his might on Roy's hand, Jane duct-taped the sticking-out hands to Roy's body. Two more bags were placed over the corpse and then Jane told Brian to pick up Roy. With considerable effort, Brian did as he was told. Jane threw the shaft of the golf club into the lake.

This is all going to plan, she thought, then it started to rain. *Fuck*, she thought, *this is one of my best suits*. By the time they had got back to the cars, both of them were soaked and covered in mud. They laid Roy on the back seat of Jane's car and she quickly drove to Knox Pharma.

The plan was to leave the body in the walk-in freezer, let the rigor mortis subside and then put Roy into one of the medical waste drums. The drums for medical waste from Knox Pharma were incinerated on a weekly basis. The next incineration was scheduled in two days, Ian knew. Brian placed Roy's body at the back of the walk-in freezer and hid it from sight with a few of the empty waste drums. Relieved that the first part of the plan had gone well, Jane instructed Brian to get in and she drove away. From a corner of the loading dock, Jose emerged and made a note in his little black book with his Parker pen.

As she drove away, Jane thought she saw someone in her rearview mirror, froze for a second, then thought, *It can't be*, and carried on. She looked down at her clothes then over at Brian. They were covered in mud and also some of Roy's blood. She looked at her watch. Just over an hour to go of Knoxate. Jane drove them to her place that was close by.

The laundry room was just off the entrance from the garage. Jane stripped off all her clothes and threw them in the washing machine, ignoring the dry-clean-only labels. Stark naked, she turned to Brian. He was simply looking at her with an inane grin. Without the Knoxate, she thought this would be a lecherous grin. "Strip off everything and put it all in there."

"Yes, Jane."

Unable to stop herself, Jane watched. Brian really had the body of an Adonis. He was well muscled and obviously worked hard on his body. Brian slipped off his boxer shorts then stood looking at Jane for the next instruction. Jane was momentarily speechless, *This guy is a perfect male,* she thought. She had seen men naked before, but Brian's penis was the biggest she had ever seen. Thick and muscular like his arms — Jane couldn't take her eyes off it. It truly was like a third arm just hanging there limply, however much bigger than most when she had seen when they were hard. *Oh my god,* she thought, *I wonder what it would look like ...*

Before she had time to quash the thought, the words came out her mouth. "Play with yourself, Brian."

He complied with a "Yes, Jane," and started to masturbate.

Jane knew what she was doing was wrong but she couldn't stop herself. She just watched in awe. It got even bigger. "Oh my God, that's impressive." Again, Jane's actions and words overrode the sensible parts of Jane's brain. She snatched a quick look at her watch on top of the washing machine.

"Brian, kiss me."

"Yes, Jane." said Brian.

"Touch me here."

"Yes, Jane."

"And here."

"Yes, Jane."

"Oh, and there!"

"Yes, Jane."

"Lick me here."

"Yes, Jane."

"Keep going,"

"Yes, Jane," said Brian, slightly muffled.

"Yes, yes, keep going!"

"Yes, Jane."

Jane grabbed Brian by the side of head. She looked him in the eye. Jane had a wild look in her eyes. Brian had an inane grin on his face and a simple 'wanting to please' look in his eyes. The laundry room floor was cold and hard. Jane didn't care. Jane was sweaty and panting.

"Brian, fuck me."

"Yes, Jane."

Over the next twenty minutes, Brian followed Jane's every command exactly. It was the best sex she had ever had. Laying there panting on the floor of the laundry room, Jane felt very bad and very good all at the same time. *If only a man listened like that all the time.* The naked Brian, panting from the exertion, looked at Jane for his next command. The rational and sensible part of Jane's brain took over again. She told Brian to take a quick shower then return. When Brian returned, looking magnificent and clean, she took his clothes from the washing machine. They did not have time to dry the clothes. It had started to rain outside.

Jane knew that Brian lived quite close by, "Brian, put these on and then run home. When you get home, take these clothes off and go straight to sleep."

"Yes, Jane." Brian dressed and ran off.

Once Brian had gone, Jane got in the shower. She still had a warm sensual feeling throughout her body but was mad at herself for being so weak and potentially messing up the plan. As the water cascaded around her, thoughts of Brian's amazing body and penis came to the fore. She groaned, not from excitement but from reality. In about fifteen minutes, the Knoxate would wear off and Brian's real brain would take over. She thought about Brian's personality. Soon the ego, the arrogance and the stupid comments would take over Brian. These thoughts brought her crashing back to earth. As she dried herself off, she said aloud, "What a shame" and "never again." Looking over at her phone, she saw Ian had texted eleven times. No way was she going to tell Ian the whole story.

She replied to his text, "Went like a dream, sleep well, talk tomorrow." All of the night's exertions had made Jane very tired. She slept very well that night.

Long Term Plan

Ian had pored over Roy's phone. It was quite a treasure trove of information. Following the text and email conversations of Roy, Ian was amazed how devious Roy was. He played one person against another and had no compunction in dumping someone in it, as long as Roy Knox gained in some way. In some ways Ian admired the skill with which Roy manipulated people, in others he was disgusted with the total lack of compassion Roy had for anyone but himself. The pragmatic, logical side of Ian took over. He was well aware of the potential trouble they were in. However loathsome Roy Knox had been, taking a life and covering it up was still a crime. Ian read everything on Roy's phone, digested it and, like the feeling of putting on cold wet clothes, he started to become Roy.

The digital communications using email and text were Ian's first foray into the life of Roy Knox. Initially, he was far too polite, but he soon learned to be much ruder and brusquer. Jane had seen to the extraction of Roy's body and tomorrow if all went well that piece of the puzzle would disappear. However, Holger at Jethro Pharm was proving to be very insistent about talking and indeed meeting up with Roy. He had somehow managed to convince the Jethro board that Knoxate was back on the books, and Ian masquerading as Roy via email and text was not able to deter the very persistent Holger. Even a "fuck off and leave me alone" email sent from Roy's phone had had no effect. Ian closed his eyes, sat back and went into deep thought. When he opened his eyes, he frowned quizzically to himself and muttered, "It could work" under his breath.

Jane woke up feeling rested and energized. She surprised herself about not feeling bad about taking advantage of Brian. In a way she knew it was rape. He did not consent. However, she had convinced herself that Brian would consent if given the opportunity to do so. Deciding not to think further about this somewhat convoluted logic, she analyzed the events and purpose of the night before. She had willingly taken part in a crime by removing and setting in place the disappearance of Roy's body. Again, she had surprised herself on how nonchalant she was about this. Jane had always considered herself a person of high morals. Perhaps these didn't apply to a pig like Roy Knox was the best explanation she came up with. She had confidence in the ability of Ian, via Roy's phone, to keep the rights of Knoxate within the company and in a few days the body of Roy Knox would simply disappear. Who would actually run the company had not been explicitly discussed, but that she would discuss at a later point, with Ian. Her phone rang and she listened to Ian at first with interest and finished the phone call with a frown. "Really, you think that will work? Mmmhh, let's meet." Jane hung up, got dressed and headed into work.

After an hour of discussion with Ian, Jane was still not sure such a crazy plan would work, but she had to admit it was the only plan they had. They had to get rid of the annoying influence of Holger at Jethro Pharma.

At the end of the day, Jane sent a text to Brian. "Fancy coffee?"

Brian was even more impressed when Jane actually brought the coffee to him. He was always excited and nervous in the presence of Jane. He just couldn't relax and be himself. Maybe he wanted to be a different person for her. Whenever he thought about her his mind got all fogged up. He had even noticed that sometimes he had memory blanks after meeting Jane. It was starting to make him worried. *Maybe it was just nerves*, he thought. Jane was making small talk and happened to mention the weather. Brian, who was hanging on her every word, looked outside. Full of guilt, Jane zapped him with the laser as he looked away. Brian paused for a second, then an inane grin appeared on his face.

"Follow me," Jane said as she left the office.

"Yes, Jane."

Ian had chosen a conference room closest to the loading dock for logistical reasons. He was nervous about the plan but was surprised just how confident he felt. It was a crazy plan, but they had to close Holger and the people at Jethro out. They had demanded an in-person meeting with Roy and simply would not give up.

If they wanted Roy Knox, then they would get Roy Knox! Ian had arranged a meeting for most employees on the other side of the building from the loading dock. For this plan to work, no prying eyes were needed. At that moment, Jane opened the door to the conference room, looking worried. Brian followed her in wearing an inane grin and carrying the lifeless body of Roy Knox over his shoulder. *Showtime*, Ian thought.

The videoconference facilities at Knox Pharma were a favorite medium that Roy had used to do business. Roy Knox loved to see himself on screen. Brian was instructed to place Roy in a chair and Jane set about Roy's face with makeup. Ian, showing a remarkable lack of scruples, attached small fishing hooks into Roy's upper lip and hands. The hooks were attached to fishing line. The fishing lines were then attached to small pieces of wood dowel. Ian explained that as a child he had become quite adept at playing with puppets and was convinced this could work. Stood on a small stepladder, Ian tried out the really quite gross marionette.

Once again, Jane was struck how obnoxious Roy could be even in death. In the conference room, this bizarre charade would have not convinced anyone, however, on screen even Jane could see there was a chance they could pull this off.

"Let's do it," said Ian. Jane was impressed how, under a stressful situation, Ian became a pillar of strength, something she would have never of expected from the shrew-like nerdy guy Ian usually was. In addition, Ian's impersonation of Roy's voice was really quite impressive. Ian practiced combining his impersonation of Roy's voice and moving his body parts. Initially the image was not one of re-animation and the fact that some of the strings broke leaving Roy with an Elvis-like snarl also detracted from the overall impression. However, after five to ten minutes of practice, and the use of stronger fishing line, Ian started to improve. Roy Knox was "alive" again.

Jane stood by the side of the video conference screen to get the best impression of what the Jethro executives would see; she was nauseated and pleased at the same time. Brian simply sat staring at Jane with an inane grin on face. "Brian, guard the door and let no one in."

"Yes, Jane."

Apart from the inane grin, Brian in this state was the perfect man, Jane thought.

"I am ready," Ian announced, appearing uncharacteristically confident, even arrogant.

He really is becoming Roy Knox, Jane thought. She hit the button and started the videoconference. *No turning back now*, she thought.

Holger and the rest of the Jethro executive team appeared on screen. "How the fuck are you guys?" Ian's opening gambit playing Roy proved effective. In fact, Ian became Roy over the next thirty minutes. When Ian set about a task, he devoured it. The mannerisms, voice and sheer rudeness of Roy Knox were really quite impressive. The Jethro board could hardly get a word in. The marionette of Roy with Ian pulling the strings took over the meeting by being boastful, rude, and arrogant. When Ian played a part, he was a method actor. "So, as you see I just really want to do this myself, so just fuck off." The parting line was classic Roy Knox.

Jane ended the video call and ran over to hug Ian as he got down from the step ladder. "You were brilliant," she exclaimed.

Still playing the role of Roy Knox, Ian took the chance to grab Jane's ass. "Thanks, babe." His lecherous smile was wiped off by a crisp slap around the face from Jane. Ian immediately reverted to being Ian, went beet red and apologized.

Jane's features softened and she smiled. "You got quite into playing Roy, I see, no big deal." She gave Ian a peck on the cheek.

Ian looked at his watch and nodded at Brian, who stood guarding the door wearing his inane grin. "Not long left."

Jane took charge. "Ian, you clean up here." Ian savagely ripped the fishing line from Roy's body parts. Shocked by the ferocity of Ian's behavior, Jane paused a while. They had both become very comfortable with violence in the last few weeks, she thought. "Brian,"

"Yes, Jane."

"Grab the body and come with me."

"Yes, Jane." Jane led Brian, carrying Roy's lifeless body, to the loading dock and was instructing Brian to place the body in a sixty-gallon drum when she heard a whiney irritating voice she had come to detest.

"I knew you guys were up to something, and now I have proof." Tommy Turner held his phone wearing a triumphant smile. "All those messages from Roy were just not like him. I knew something was up, you are going to jail for this bitch." Tommy turned and started to walk out of the loading dock. He was stopped by a punch in the face from Ian. The two men, neither of them athletes, traded ineffectual punches, then wrestled each other up against some storage boxes. Both men were out of shape and both breathing heavily.

"You're going to fucking jail! You fucking killed my friend Roy," Tommy was yelling. "Maybe you can get together with your fag boyfriend Justin."

Ian stopped and simply stared at Tommy, now he knew who had taken the pictures. Ian attacked Tommy with renewed vigor and ferocity. Unfortunately, as he charged, he tripped, careening headlong towards Tommy. Never a man to pass up an opportunity, Tommy kneed Ian in the head, laying him out cold. Tommy glanced back at Jane, triumphant, and headed for the loading room door.

Jane's mind was a blank, then she suddenly crystalized on a solution. "Brian, get him."

"Yes, Jane."

Tommy looked worried and started to run. He was no match for Brian and knew it. However, he did have a good head start on Brian and could maybe get through the door and lock it to get away.

Jane had watched the fight between Ian and Tommy, frozen and shocked. She now wished she had thought about getting Brian involved earlier. Her brain was calculating the distance between Tommy and the door, then Brian to Tommy. Brian had been instructed to "get him" but had not been instructed to do it quickly so he was simply walking towards Tommy with an inane grin on his face. "Fucking run."

"Yes, Jane." Brian obeyed and quickened his pace.

He is not going to get him in time, Jane thought. The horror of all of this being made public suddenly hit Jane all at once. What had she done? Tommy had almost made it to the door, Brian was now running and gaining quickly, but he was not going to get to Tommy before he got to the door.

All of a sudden, Tommy stopped in his tracks. Jane could not see why; Brian's body blocked her view. Jane stepped sideways to get a better view. Brian arrived at the immobile Tommy and simply held him in place. She walked over to see what was going on. From in front of the two men stepped Jose, wiping blood off his Parker pen with a handkerchief. Jane was shocked to see Jose — where the hell had he come from? She then looked at Tommy who had a puncture wound in the middle of his body and his shirt was covered in blood. Jane then looked down at Jose's hand and pen, both covered in blood. However, Jose was meticulously and nonchalantly cleaning both. Jose had obviously rammed his pen up between Tommy's ribs and punctured his heart, killing Tommy almost instantaneously.

"But… how… where?" Jane couldn't finish her thoughts as so many were whirling in her mind. She looked from Tommy to Jose to Brian. Brian was smiling inanely, Tommy, never an attractive man, wore a shocked look but the color was quickly draining from his face.

Jose returned Jane's stare then in a measured voice said, "I like working here. Cannot jeopardize that. I like you, you run the company. Now we have to get rid of these two," he said, waving his hands at Tommy and Roy. Jose addressed Brian. "Put Tommy in that drum."

"Yes, Jose."

"You clear this up. Pickup of medical waste is Monday, I will keep people away from here… okay… okay, Dr Porrima?" Jose was always very respectful.

"Erm yes… thank you, but…" Jose held up his hand and exited the loading dock.

Jane stood for a second trying to fathom what had just happened. She was awakened from her thoughts by Ian groaning. She then looked at her watch, then in horror at Brian. His inane grin was there but seemed to be disappearing. "Run home, Brian," was all Jane could think of. Brian paused a while, frowned but then thankfully complied. Jane made sure the tops of the sixty-gallon drums were on tight, found a hose, and hosed Tommy's blood from the loading dock floor, then helped Ian to his feet.

"What happened?" asked Ian, looking scared and confused.

"Let's get out of here and I will tell you all."

Pact

Brian had stopped running halfway home. He was unsure why he was running and couldn't recall the last few hours. He just had Jane's voice in his head. "Run home, Brian." What had he done? Why was he so confused around her? Why did he have memory blanks? Was this love? Brian was in a completely new territory with his feelings. His usual attitude to women was easy come, easy go, plenty more fish in the sea. This was totally different. A new young woman had started at Knox Pharma, she was Brazilian who was incredibly cute, a great figure and had even flirted with Brian. Cassia was surprised her ample curvy assets had not turned Brian's head. Indeed, he looked distracted when talking to her. This was unusual, and she wondered if Brian was gay. However, she hadn't noticed that Jane had walked by when they were chatting in the lab. Under normal circumstances, Brian would have made many comments, flirted and at definitely made a play for Cassia. He was lost. He always knew what to do, he always knew what he wanted, and now everything was a mess in his head. Brian sat down on the side of the road and did something he hadn't done in years... he cried.

"We need a drink." Jane hadn't asked it as a question, more as a demand. Ian complained that his clothes were covered in blood and he couldn't go to a bar or home looking like this. They went to Jane's apartment and while his clothes washed, Ian sat in Jane's bathrobe and listened to what had happened.

Ian was back to being Ian, no more acting like Roy. He sat and listened quietly, though a little embarrassed about being in his underwear and Jane's robe in her apartment. He was not sure of many of his feelings with regards sexuality, but he knew one thing — he loved Jane. However, he was pretty sure his love for Jane was more like a sister than a lover. Deep down, he was still very hurt about the photo between him and Justin and wondered if Jane knew or had questions. If she did, she was sensitive enough not to pry. Ian asked a few questions about the night's events for clarification and sat for a long time to think. The pink fluffy bathrobe felt rather comfortable and soft against his skin, allowing him to relax a little and think.

"So, Jose was just there and he...?"

"Yep, and then nonchalantly walked off," Jane cut in. Jane was on her second glass of wine. She refilled Ian's glass as he went back into thought. Jane had never been so scared in her life when it looked like Tommy was going to get away and spill everything to whoever would listen. Now she couldn't help but feel exhilarated and excited. *Have we just got away with it?* she wondered. The two obstacles to developing Knoxate properly and under their control were Roy Knox and Jethro. Both were now dead and buried. Well, technically Roy was dead, in a plastic barrel waiting for incineration, but close enough. The Tommy incident had been a close call, thanks to Jose — wow what an enigma he was — they were free, weren't they?

Jane looked at Ian. He was gazing at the wall, obviously in deep thought. He looked rather silly in her fluffy pink bathrobe and he certainly wasn't the man of her dreams, but she realized quite how strongly she loved him, not in a sexual way just like a … brother. The thought caught Jane off guard. She had been an only child and always dreamed of a brother or sister, and now she had her wish. Ian got up and started strolling up and down her apartment, still in deep thought. As he walked by Jane, she suddenly reached out and gave Ian a big hug. Ian was completely caught off guard and pushed himself away. He fell backward onto the sofa revealing a rather fetching pair of red Calvin Klein underwear. Jane observed Ian with amusement. He was a lovely man but just so awkward with almost everything.

Ian quickly wrapped the robe around himself. "What the hell are you doing?" he exclaimed in a voice that was a little too shrill to be effective.

Jane simply smiled, then said, "I just wanted to give you a hug. We have been through a lot together."

"Oh." Ian looked more relaxed.

"And you were grabbing my ass about one hour ago," Jane teased. giving herself an ass squeeze.

Once again Ian blushed and murmured, "That was the Roy persona, not me."

"I know." Jane leant over and kissed Ian on the forehead. Ian didn't blush or resist or look awkward; he simply smiled. Jane sat down next to Ian. "Whatever we decide, we are both in this up to our necks, so we are in it together, agree?"

"Agreed."

They finished another bottle of wine, causing Ian to call his parents and tell them he was not coming home, and discussed the strategy going forward all night. When Ian awoke on Jane's sofa, he pondered the plan through the fog of his hangover. He concluded that he needed to re-assess when his head was clearer, but the plan they hatched had merit.

Clearing Up

Brian woke up unhappy and confused. Again, he had blanks in his memory. He knew he had been with Jane yesterday at work but things after that were, to say the least, a little fuzzy. *Oh my God, I am in love*, he thought. Brian had often been loved, spurned such love as it was uncomfortable, but had never actually been in love. The thought both excited and scared him. He remembered going to work, having a discussion with Jane (did he dream this?) and then then finding himself by the side of the road sweaty from running. This feeling of lack of control was alien to Brian and he didn't like it. He sat looking at his phone, thinking of Jane and wanting to call or text her, but had nothing to say. Thank God tomorrow was Saturday so he had the weekend to pull himself together. By the end of the morning, Brian had concluded that love was not worth it. It was for wimps and he would never do this again. However, every chime and boing from his phone sent him scurrying to see if it was Jane — it wasn't — his heart leapt and then sank every time.

Jane made Ian toast and coffee for breakfast. Initially silent at the table, Ian eventually spoke up. "We have to make sure the bodies are disposed of and soon."

He didn't look up while he spread more raspberry jam on his toast.

"What about Jose?" Jane was always someone who got to the point, even if the point was uncomfortable.

"Where the hell, did he come from?" Ian sounded almost annoyed.

"I didn't see him until he, errr..." Jane trailed off. The images of the previous day's gruesome events did not sit well with raspberry jam.

"It's Saturday, things will be quiet at work. We should go in and check everything out." Ian was amazed that he sounded authoritative and in command when in fact he was feeling quite nauseous and really wanted to curl up in a little ball.

Jane agreed. They both dressed and drove to work, both of them contemplative with their thoughts. Jane broke the silence as they neared the loading dock of Knox pharma. "Ready for this?"

Ian simply nodded, seeming scared but with a resolute look on his face. They drove by the impeccable landscaping and parked at the loading dock.

The loading dock looked, well... it looked normal. Nothing out of place, the floors were clean and there were no signs of blood or a struggle. For a moment Jane thought maybe this had been all a dream. She had briefly washed the blood away with a hose but surely things wouldn't be this clean. Jane cast her mind back to the previous day's escapades. Empty drums and boxes had been knocked over in the struggles between

Tommy and Brian. These had been all cleaned up. Jose must have stayed around and cleaned up all the mess.

"Who is this guy?" and "What does he want?" went through Jane's mind.

"There." Ian walked over to two sixty-gallon drums set slightly apart from the others. As they circled the translucent drums, any thoughts Jane had of this simply being a bad dream vanished. She could see dark objects at the bottom of each drum, strange grotesque human-like shapes. Jane shuddered and stepped back.

"Dr Porrima."

"Aaarrgghh!" Jane jumped out of her skin, landed with cat-like ease and went into attack mode. The person who had talked to her was standing right behind her. She executed a perfect reverse kick aimed at the man's groin. He simply stood aside and then she aimed a roundhouse kick at the man's head. He simply ducked. Jane's heart rate had already been high. Now her heart threatened to blow right out of her chest. She turned to face her assailant.

Jose was watching her, bemused. He clicked his pen and placed it in his top pocket. "What the fuck!" exclaimed Jane, feeling lightheaded.

"I am cleaning up. Leave this to me," Jose said nonchalantly with a shrug of his shoulders.

Ian was still in awe of the super athletic martial arts moves Jane had just pulled off and equally in awe with the apparent ease with which Jose had evaded them.

"Erm, Jose, we need to talk," Ian stammered. "This really is our…"

Jose cut him off with a raised hand. "You are good people. I like you. This guy, both of them," he said waving in the direction of the drums, "were bad, and they deserved to die."

"I now work for you," Jose said pointing at both Jane and Ian.

"Oh," was all Ian could reply.

Jane needed to pee. "I will be back," she said as she turned away. She also needed to think and sit down. Jose and Ian just looked at each other.

When Jane returned, she found Ian helping Jose place one of the drums on a handcart. "Jose thinks we should burn the bodies," came Ian's reply to Jane's quizzical look. "The incinerator is on and best not to wait until Monday." Jane watched as the two men struggled, rolling the handcart up the ramp of the incinerator.

A laboratory is a wonderful place to commit murder and get away with it, Jane mused.

Once at the top of the ramp, Jose opened the safety gate, and the barrel bounced down the entry to the mouth of the incinerator. However, the bounce caused the barrel to get stuck sideways in the mouth.

Showing remarkable agility for someone who was not agile, Ian jumped over the gate and calmly walked down the entryway. "I will just give it a push," he said, just as he showed his true nonathletic colors and tripped up. All images of Ian's agility were long gone as he hurtled headfirst and arms waving towards the mouth of the flaming incinerator. Ian's head smashed into the barrel, dislodging it and causing it to fall into the incinerator. Luckily, Ian's right arm had lodged on a guard rail. For the second time in two days, Ian had a headache and a head injury.

Jose calmly walked around the gangway and helped Ian off the equipment. "Maybe you could help me, Dr. Porrima," Jose said almost pleadingly with Jane.

"Sure." The second barrel was loaded and disposed of with much less fuss than the first.

Ian sat on the floor nursing yet another black eye. Although both eyes were swelling, Ian could see the black belching smoke coming out of the incinerator chimney. "So much for our clean air policy," Ian mumbled to himself.

Jane helped Ian to his feet and then tuned to face Jose. "So you work for us? What does that mean, exactly?"

"I like you, I work for you." Jose was a man of few words, something that appealed to Jane.

However, she pushed on. "You know this is illegal, all of this." She waved her arms around.

"God has a plan that is above the law," was all Jose offered in return. He turned to close the door of the incinerator. "Now these two are gone, I work for you, okay?"

Jane nodded and looked at Ian. "Erm, sure." Ian was acutely aware that they had just committed and covered up two murders and were currently discussing this as calmly as one would a take-out order. Jose walked back into the building and disappeared. Ian turned to look directly at Jane.

"What?" she said irritably. She knew Ian was looking for direction but was hoping he would provide some. He simply stood there, looking away then looking back at her. "Fuck, okay, I guess the one with the vagina takes charge as always." Jane stormed off in the direction of the car.

Ian paused for a second then scurried after her. Jane got in the car, opened the door for Ian and then sat for a long time thinking. Ian was afraid to say anything, so he closed his eyes and did what he did best — analyze the situation.

Jane eventually spoke in a much warmer tone. "Sorry about snapping at you back there."

"That's okay, replied Ian. "Over the last few months, we have purposefully controlled people against their will, had a hand in two murders and covered them up by burning the bodies." He paused, "You have a lot on your mind." Ian smiled, "So what now?"

Jane didn't need reminding of the predicament they were in and felt like punching Ian in the mouth. However, Ian's sweet smile and pleading look placated Jane. "Can we do this? Can we get away with this? Can we take over the company?" Jane's questions came gushing out just as Ian had gushed the all too obvious facts.

Ian sat for a moment and then replied, "Yes we can."

Over the next hour or so Ian and Jane planned. Ian was still acting via Roy's phone. As Roy, he could slowly, so as not to arise suspicion, transfer authority away from Roy and over to Jane. Jane had queried Ian as to why her, and not him. The simply reply was that Ian felt she was the stronger leader. They both agreed upon the outline of the plan and said they would meet again Monday to discuss. Ian said he wanted to go home as he had a headache and his mother was asking how he was doing. The explanation for his face was going to be he had fallen down when drunk, a bit feeble but their collective brain power was ebbing. Jane drove Ian home.

When they got there, Ian asked about Brian. "He must be confused. What shall we do?"

Jane had forgotten all about Brian. "Oh shit, Brian. Leave him to me," was Jane's reply.

Brian woke up Saturday, late, still confused and a little scared. His memory loss of the previous day and this novel feeling of yearning for Jane caused him alarm. So, Brian did what he always did when he needed to think — he went to the gym. Headphones on, loud music and the pleasure of pumping iron — this was just what he needed. Some of the friends at the gym had approached him to say hi but quickly retreated when they could see the singular purpose in his face. No pain, no gain. Brian put himself through a grueling set of workouts. Every muscle in his body was screaming and bulging. He showered, allowing the pain from the work-out to numb his frayed nerves. His phone chirped.

"Want a coffee?" The text came from Jane. His heart leapt and then sank. He was elated and scared to meet her all at the same time. Of course, he agreed to meet her.

Jane gave him a big hug when they met at the coffee shop. Brian immediately started to get aroused and excused himself to go to the bathroom, where he slapped himself very hard across the face and told himself to pull it together. A man heading toward the urinal looked in his direction and headed to one of the stalls making sure the door was looked. The sight of a very large muscular man slapping himself was rather disconcerting.

Jane said she would order the coffees and watched Brian as he hurried to the bathroom. *What a hunk of meat*, she thought. The veins on his biceps were bulging more than usual, the workout had made him even hotter than normal. She could only imagine the rest of him.

"Is that all?" the young man behind the counter asked. Jane was aware she was biting her bottom lip and not paying attention. Flushing red immediately, she paid and found a table. Brian came back with a large red mark on his right cheek, Jane decided to say nothing. Brian was wearing a tight white T-shirt, and his chest and arm muscles could clearly be defined. Jane mentally slapped herself to stop this nonsense and concentrate.

"I was worried about you yesterday. You said you had a headache and then disappeared?" Jane ventured. She left the question open ended, hoping he would elaborate.

Brian was quiet for a while. He was so drawn to Jane it hurt, but he just couldn't tell her how he felt. "I think I have a brain tumor."

"What?" Jane was bemused — not the reply she was expecting.

Brian repeated his claim and then substantiated it by saying he had been having memory lapses. With a little prodding, Jane explored Brian's version of events over the last few days. She was relieved to find out that Brian did not have a clue about certain events. Brian finished with him running along the road and having no idea of how he got there. He finally looked Jane straight in the eye. He almost said something and then stopped himself.

Jane was touched by Brian's emotion. Deep down there was a kind and gentle man underneath all of that bluster and male pride. She saw a way to temper his worries. "I don't think it is a brain tumor, I would chalk it up to stress. We have all been working very hard. In fact, funny you should say this, I also have had some memory lapses."

Jane could see this deception was working. Brian seemed to brighten. His eyes jumped between her own and her cleavage. The more she talked and made him feel better, the longer his eyes stayed on her cleavage. Normally annoyed by such behavior — she had been ogled since her breasts had first appeared — Jane would have normally said something to embarrass the perpetrator. However, this behavior was now turning her on. She found herself moving from his eyes down towards his chest. Mentally she kept slapping herself and telling herself no, but things were stirring inside of her. *Just one more time and that is it,* she told herself. "I am a little hungry. Want a cookie?" Jane ventured.

"Oh, I will get it, you got the coffees." Brian bounced up and Jane watched his perfectly formed butt cheeks head off to the counter.

"Just one more time," she murmured as she popped a pill in what was left of Brian's coffee. Shortly thereafter, Jane enquired "isn't that so and so?" pointing behind Brian. As Brian turned, she zapped him. Brian paused for a second then turned to Jane with an inane grin on his face. "Drive to my place."

"Yes, Jane."

Over the next few hours Jane had the most fulfilling, acrobatic, and energetic sex of her whole life. She lost count of the number of times she had orgasmed. They had done it in the hallway, in the kitchen, up against the aquarium (she would clean the water up later, sorry fish), on top of the washing machine and finally in the bed. Jane laid there panting, exhausted but totally fulfilled. Brian was laid on his side looking at her with an inane grin. Amazingly, he still had an erection, Jane admired its perfect form and her eyes took in his amazingly chiseled body. She thought for a while, checked her watch then said, "Brian, get dressed and go home."

"Yes Jane"

Taking Over

Monday morning Jane and Ian sat in the board room and filled on the details of the plan they had hatched over the weekend. Roy was going to take a leave of absence and visit a Caribbean island. Ian (acting as Roy) would then systematically move ownership of all Knox concerns over to the new CEO, Dr. Jane Porrima. Ian would lead the scientific and clinical aspects of Knox Pharma as its new chief scientific officer. Tang had initially put up some resistance to Ian. However, after a few weeks of no snide or rude remarks, Tang soon fell into line and wondered at the contrast between his old boss, Roy, and his newer and much nicer boss, Ian.

The workload was intense and both Ian and Jane spent long hours getting Knoxate off the ground and into clinical trials. They both had time for little else. Roy Knox became a thing of the past. Indeed, when the notice came that Roy had retired due to an illness, there was no celebration, no consternation, just a sense of good riddance to bad rubbish.

There was a brief moment of alarm when the police had come looking for Tommy Turner. However, it turned out they were investigating Tommy for allegations of blackmail and some rather unsavory photos Tommy had taken. Jane had noticed how quiet Ian had become when the police had interviewed them. After the interview, Ian had looked embarrassed and sad. That afternoon he locked himself in his office and Jane decided it best not to bother him. As she well knew, things concerning Roy Knox and Tommy Turner were best left in the past.

It really seemed as if they had gotten away with it. Jane had stopped thinking of the events as murder, and more as obstacles that had to be overcome. This helped her "deal with it," she told herself. All of the Knox Pharma staff had been working all hours to produce and get Knoxate to clinical trials. They had cut all of their ties to Jethro Pharma and fended off multiple other bids. Jane had occasionally been aware of Brian's eyes following her around at work but they were both too busy to address anything. Brian's memory lapses had seemed to disappear and after a few months he felt he was back to his normal self.

Ian had completely thrown himself into work and was loving it. *This is "it",* he thought. He was in charge of a great research project; the work was exciting and the team looked to him for inspiration. Weekend or weekdays, it didn't matter, Ian became consumed by his work and he had never been happier. He had always felt as though there was something missing. That something for him was a purpose and Knoxate gave him that purpose. A room next to Roy's old office had been converted into his own office. He and Jane consulted on everything. The work was moving along at a frantic pace and no one had time to dwell on the past. This suited Ian just fine. The visit from the police and ensuing discussion about Tommy Turner had proven very difficult day for Ian. He had tried very hard to forget anything about those photos of Justin and himself. The questions about Tommy had brought it all flooding back. He was so embarrassed and spent the whole afternoon in his office simply staring out of the window and crying. How could he have been so stupid? He had been thankful that Jane had given him space and realized that they were definitely in sync with each other's feelings. They were a great team. He had seen the video of Jane undressing on Roy's phone, well part of it, so suspected Roy had also tried awful things with Jane. He had deleted the video and would never tell Jane about it. Life was so good, he vowed never to look into the past and only into the future.

Jane walked out of her office feeling tired but in great spirits. The endless amounts of coffee caused Jane to take a visit to the bathroom. On the way out, she bumped into Liz.

"Oh, my God, how are you? Hardly see you these days."

"I know, I am sorry, been super busy." Jane was embarrassed that she had not spent time with her friend.

"How are things, anything new?" Jane enquired.

Liz pulled her into a corner of the bathroom. She bent over and checked the other stalls were empty. "I fucked Brian," Liz exclaimed.

Jane was intrigued. "Really? I thought you hated him." Jane was surprised she felt a pang of jealousy. "I know he can be a real prick, but he is soo hot."

"Remember the celebration we had after Knoxate entered clinical trials?"

"Yes," said Jane.

"Well, a few drinks and one thing led to another." Liz was smiling. "And let me tell you something else. Not only does he have a great body, he is a tripod. Massive cock." Liz made expansive motions with her arms. "Oh my god."

Liz then frowned. "However, I think it is too big."

"Really?" Jane was intrigued. She remembered Brian's cock and it was perfect for her.

"Yeah," said Liz. "He kept going all floppy, maybe it is too big to get enough blood supply, so bit of a downer there."

Jane found herself smiling and feeling quite pleased. *A strange way to feel,* she thought.

"However, maybe just nerves. I hope to try out the tripod again sometime soon," said Liz, winking and giggling. "Maybe go all the way." Liz and Jane exchanged a few more updates and then were interrupted when another woman came in to use the restroom.

Jane walked back to her office, feeling very pleased. *Mmmhh, Brian couldn't get it up for Liz, but boy oh boy, could he get it up for me,* she thought. Jane felt a little bad for her friend and the fact that she was gloating over her. However, she simply put it down to her competitive spirit. As she walked into Roy's old office, now her office, she told Mary no calls for the next half hour. She sat down in the large leather chair, spun it around and laughed. She was exquisitely happy. Jane was well respected by her team. She treated them well and in return they respected her. No one tried to look down her blouse, well not often, and no one made lewd comments about her looks. She had fought her looks all her life and wanted recognition for her brain, not her boobs. Her hard work and determination in getting Knoxate into clinical trials had impressed all of those around her. She felt their respect when they had team meetings. Jane was happy and fulfilled. *This is "it",* Jane thought. *This is what I have been looking for.* She sat spinning for a while longer before the intercom buzzed. Mary's voice informed her that her three-thirty had arrived. Jane welcomed her three-thirty with a smile.

Jose performed his rounds. Both Jane and Ian had tried to engage him in conversation about "the incident" and he had waved them away. "I work for you. I am happy," was his only reply. Jose knew everything that went on at Knox Pharma. He liked it that way.

He found himself at the loading dock, made his inspection and as he walked by the incinerator, he looked up and smiled. Jose paused for a second and reflected on his life. "This is it," he said to himself. It had been a long road from Colombia, but now he was at a place where he felt he belonged. The employees at Knox Pharma were his family. He looked after them and in return they gave him their gratitude and respect. Everyone knew Jose here and he received many smiles, waves and hellos as he made his rounds. Yes, Jose was very happy here and no one was going to mess with his adopted family. His eyes turned away from the incinerator chimney. He pulled his Parker pen from his inside pocket, made a notation in his little book and carried on his rounds with a smile on his face.